AF442358

Montana HEAT

JOSIE JADE

Copyright © 2024 by Calamittie Jane Publishing

All rights reserved.

No part of this book may be reproduced in any form or by any electronic or mechanical means, including information storage and retrieval systems, without written permission from the author, except for the use of brief quotations in a book review.

This a work of fiction. Names, characters, places, and incidents are the product of the author's imagination or are used fictitiously, and any resemblance to actual persons, living or dead, business establishments, events or locals is entirely coincidental.

Cover created by Deranged Doctor Designs.

A Calamittie Jane Publishing Book

MONTANA HEAT: RESTING WARRIOR RANCH

Prologue

Jensen Chambers

One year ago

"I'm not a mechanic, Lucas. You know that, right?"

Lucas Everett turned and grinned at me as we walked through the empty automotive repair garage in Garnet Bend, Montana.

"Only in that you never formally went to school for it. You were always tinkering with engines when we were kids. By the time we graduated, you could fix anything on wheels, and you know it."

I shrugged, walking around the place, appreciating the tools and equipment that would've made the repairs I'd done as a teen so much easier. As it was, I'd made do since I could do a lot of work on my friends' vehicles and make good money at it.

Friends Lucas had introduced me to when I'd moved in next door to him at fifteen.

Most boys Lucas's age didn't want to have anything to do with a kid who had been kicked around the foster system and had arrived at his new family's house with his shit in a garbage bag.

Teens were brutal, and most of them had been happy to make fun of my lack of family and belongings.

Not Lucas. He'd walked over the first day I'd arrived and asked if I wanted to shoot some hoops. And then had never left me behind. Not once. Not ever.

Even as we'd grown and gone different directions in life, we'd stayed close. Lucas was a brother in every way but blood.

"Okay, yeah, I have some innate skills when it comes to vehicles. But I have a job. So I don't know why you brought me out here."

He pushed a rolling tool tray a little farther off to the side. "You have a job you hate."

"Eh. Hate is a strong word. I like the security field."

"But you don't like being middle management."

I studied the vehicle lift in front of me. It was in good shape. "That's true. Middle management sucks ass."

Lucas chuckled. "And studying surveillance screens until your eyes blur then writing five point two million reports per week isn't much better."

I walked over and crouched down in front of an air compressor. It looked to be in pretty good shape. "Also true."

"Last time you visited the ranch, I tried to talk you into staying, but you said you weren't a cowboy."

I snickered without looking at him. "Still aren't. Animals aren't my thing."

"I get it, man. You didn't feel like there was a place for you. We'll probably never get you up on a horse. This garage would create a place for you here. You could do what you love."

"I don't know that being a mechanic is what I love."

He leaned up against the wall. "What you love is working with your hands. But more than that, Jensen, this is a chance for you to work for *yourself*. To own something outright. I know how much that means to you. You were talking about an investment last time you visited. This could be it."

As much as I didn't like my security job—and Lucas was right, being at other people's beck and call had never been what I wanted—it had always paid well. And from there, I'd saved and grown a successful stock portfolio.

"When I said investment, I meant in the Resting Warrior Ranch. Helping you guys help more people."

What Lucas and the guys did there was impressive. *Important.* Training service and emotional support animals to help people suffering from PTSD? Offering them a chance to recover through the healing freedom of the Montana range?

I wanted to be part of that in whatever way I could.

"We don't want your money."

I stood and wiped my hands on my pants. "And fuck you very much, too."

Lucas laughed. I loved hearing it. Loved how falling in love with his wife Evelyn, having a kid and another on the way, had brought out so much more laughter in him.

"What I mean—" Lucas shook his head "—is that we'd rather have you here than just have your money. This place may be the answer to that."

Lucas had already told me the story. The place had been sitting empty for months since the bank reclaimed it after the previous owner did some shady shit and ended up in jail.

Shady shit being almost killing Jude Williams and his woman, Lena.

"It's an amazing price. Having it back on its feet would help the town, plus the guys and I would know you're nearby if we need backup for anything."

I looked around some more. I definitely enjoyed working with my hands. I had a love for taking things apart to see how they worked then putting them back together. Every time I did that, I felt complete. A sense of accomplishment. When everything else in the world seemed unknown or prone to change, the fundamental process of fixing something—rebuilding it—calmed me.

It didn't take a psychological genius to know all that stemmed from growing up in the foster care system.

"If I did it, we would need to completely overhaul the place. Get rid of the bad juju for Lena and Jude. Make it something new."

"Make it something yours," he added.

"Yeah. That too."

"The guys have already been coming up with designs for possible remodels in case you said yes."

I looked over at my friend, shaking my head. "Pretty confident in your ability to convince me, aren't you?"

He walked over and slapped me on the shoulder. "Not confident. *Hopeful*. This is your chance to be part of the Resting Warrior Ranch family, Jensen. You don't have to live on the property to be one of us. You already are. Everyone feels the same."

Lucas had been family since the day I'd met him. Now, it looked like that family was about to expand a great deal.

"I'll do it."

Chapter One

Kenzie Hurst

Garnet Bend. Population 2518.

I gritted my teeth as I drove by the sign outside the tiny town that was about to become my home.

Temporary home.

Temporary. Please, God, please, please, please: temporary.

Because I was a city girl. Hadn't ever seen the appeal of small communities—no live theater, no Michelin star restaurants, no bustle.

Hell, I was probably the only person on the planet who found Hallmark movies unbearable.

There was always a pumpkin patch or a dog or a run-down bed-and-breakfast that someone's great-aunt—that sneaky little matchmaker—had left her in the will. And a good ol' boy who'd lived next door all his life and could help her fix it up.

No shirt. Tight jeans. Tool belt.

Okay, maybe that part wasn't so bad. I mean, who didn't like a sexy shirtless guy with a tool belt?

And the bed-and-breakfast part wasn't so bad either. After all, I was a Realtor, so I could definitely see the appeal of that sort of property.

But the rest of it? Not for me.

And a town so small that it needed to make sure to include the *eighteen* in the 2,518 population sign?

That felt pretty damn small.

I officially hated Garnet Bend.

Okay, that wasn't fair. I hadn't even made it all the way into the town yet. But I definitely hated why I was here.

I hated that I had as many of my belongings as I could fit inside this car and the rest stored in the basement of my parents' house.

Beethoven's Fifth blasted from my phone, and my heart stopped at the ringtone, my hands gripping the steering wheel until my knuckles were white.

I hated that any sort of sudden noise or movement put me in near panic mode too.

I reached down and hit the speaker button on the phone.

Hated that it wasn't my regular phone.

"Hey, Mom."

"Hey, sweetie. Did you make it?"

"Just arriving." I knew my mother wanted to know exactly where I was, but she knew I couldn't tell her. Police orders.

How I felt about that?

Well, I was starting to see a pattern there.

"Is it okay? Dad and I don't like this. We don't like not knowing where you are."

"I know, Mom. But it's going to be fine."

My parents knew only the very basics of what had been happening. They knew there was trouble. They knew I'd had to leave Denver because of what had been going on.

But I'd been careful to keep the worst of it from them.

The night terrors. The constant looking over my shoulder. The fact that I could barely eat—and definitely couldn't focus.

The knowledge that I worried every day might be my last. Which seemed so melodramatic but was true.

So, I was here in Garnet Bend, with all 2,518 of its inhabitants, hoping I could get my life back.

"Are you sure you can't tell me where you are? You know Dad and I would never tell a soul."

"Not right now." I slowed my car to an acceptable speed so I could glance around the main strip as I drove through town. "It's for your own safety. Detective Watters said no one could know."

Garnet Bend seemed to have all the basics—grocery store, general store, and most importantly, a coffee shop. So, maybe I would survive.

I had to admit, the backdrop of mountains and wide-open space as far as the eye could see was truly mesmerizing—especially with the last of the fall leaves barely hanging on as winter started to close in. It looked like something out of a painting.

"It's pretty here," I continued when she didn't respond to my last statement. That meant she was perturbed. I didn't blame her; I wasn't a fan either.

Because even with the gorgeous setting, it still wasn't home.

Not that I didn't like mountains. Denver—*home*—had them all around. But Denver also had skyscrapers and ten-lane highways and tons of people milling around everywhere—all ignoring each other.

"I still don't like it," Mom said finally.

"It's just temporary, okay? Let's stay positive." I was using the last of my *positive* reserves just saying that. Normally, I wasn't a pessimist—the opposite, in fact—but I couldn't find much positive in me right now. Thus, the hatefest that had been circling my mind all day.

"I just want you safe, sweetie."

"Me too. Detective Watters said this is the best thing to do until the situation is handled."

"I know, but—"

"Let me call you back in a little while, okay?" I knew where this conversation was heading and needed to stop it while I could. "I have an appointment."

"What kind of appointment?"

I cringed. One with the police chief. Telling Mom that would not get her off the phone. "Just some settling-in stuff."

"Okay. We'll talk to you soon. Love you."

"Love you too."

"Be safe."

I disconnected the call. *Safe.* Something I had taken for granted my whole life and now was all I could think about.

Would Garnet Bend actually be the safe place Detective Watters implied? Surely I was going to stick out as a stranger. Obviously, all 2,518 people sat around and studied one another, so they'd know if an outsider was in their midst.

I let out a sigh at my own ridiculousness.

But still… I couldn't work here. I'd spent the past five years building my reputation as a commercial real estate agent, then had found a particular talent for developing seminars teaching others the nuances of the business.

I regularly taught workshops with more people in attendance than lived in all of Garnet Bend.

Stopping at a red light, I looked more closely at the town. Old-fashioned streetlamps lined the sidewalks, trash receptacles had been placed in prime traffic areas, and the businesses were nicely spaced and seemed to be thriving. Everything looked inviting and clean. Honestly, a Realtor's dream.

A brief friendly honk behind me—not the loud blare I would've gotten in Denver, so one point to Garnet Bend—jarred me out of my assessment. I looked up, noticing the light had turned green. Cringing, I lifted my hand in apology. "Sorry!"

Squaring my shoulders and taking a deep breath, I proceeded

ahead to my destination, turning into a small parking lot as it came up on my right. This was the reason I was in Garnet Bend in the first place.

Trying to stay safe from the stalker who'd decided to make my life hell.

My fist made its way to my stomach, trying to rub away the ball of stress formed there. I knew firsthand if I didn't get it to ease now, it would worsen and turn into nausea and blind panic.

It was already starting. My eyes darted around the parking lot. Looking for...what exactly, I didn't know.

And that was the problem: the not knowing.

It was a terrifying thought—that someone even now might be watching me, learning my habits, and lying in wait. But what they were waiting for, I had no clue.

I tried my best to be aware of my surroundings, stay visible when I was out, and never be the last person to leave anywhere or walk alone.

But still, I jumped at every sound, tensed when a stranger came close, and I suspected everyone. Every time I walked to my door or opened my mailbox, the possibility of something ugly always lurked in the shadows.

Really ugly. My stalker had made sure I knew that.

For weeks, anxiety had taken up residence in my stomach. It knotted now, spreading uneasiness through me even though I was safe in my vehicle. The toast and coffee I'd had for breakfast churned uncomfortably. I took a few deep breaths, hoping to keep it down.

I was not meeting the first people in my new hometown with vomit on me.

"Just get to the appointment." I swallowed hard, my mouth dry from the tension and stress of seeing strangers nearby. "One step at a time."

Detective Watters was friends with the police chief here in

Garnet Bend, which was how we'd decided this was where I would lie low since things had...*escalated* with my stalker last week.

Escalated. Such a benign word for blood being splattered on your home's walls.

But yes, a formal check-in with the police here was necessary, Watters said. Let them know who I was. It would make me feel more comfortable.

Comfort had been foreign to me for nearly four months. Somehow, I didn't think showing up here was going to make me instantly warm and cozy.

As soon as I opened my door, my stress ratcheted up. It was only a few dozen feet from my parking spot to the door, but I was über aware of my own vulnerability. Aware of what could be done to me.

My body was prepared for attack, on heightened alert. Which sounded all heroic, but it was really just exhausting.

I relaxed only slightly when I made it through the door. Not that I was truly much safer here, but I at least felt that way.

The police building wasn't big, but it seemed to employ about eighteen of the town's 2,518 residents. A few officers, assistants, secretaries.

The woman behind a counter closest to the door smiled at me. "How may I help you today?"

I stepped forward with a small wave. "I'm here to speak to the police chief. I have an appointment."

"That'd be me," a voice said from my left. "Charlie Garcia, at your service. Nice to meet you in person, Ms. Hurst." His voice was gruff, but his smile was polite, like it had been when Detective Watters and I had spoken to him on the phone a few days ago.

He gestured to the younger man standing next to him. "This is Lachlan Callaway, one of our deputies here in Garnet Bend. I've filled him in with the details of your case."

I shook both men's hands. "Kenzie, please. Thanks for meeting with me."

Charlie turned toward the hallway. "Let's go to my office. Lachlan was just heading out, but I'd like to go over some of the details with you."

Deputy Callaway tipped his head in my direction. "Don't hesitate to call if you need us while you're here. Even if it seems trivial."

That was such a refreshing change from my first meetings with the police in Denver. "Thank you."

The deputy left and Chief Garcia led me the rest of the way to his office, closing the wooden door behind him.

I tensed at the sound of the click behind me. It sounded so final. I had to tamp down my panic. I was in a police station, for crying out loud. Nothing was going to happen here.

"Ben—Detective Watters—sent the file from your case," Chief Garcia started. "And, of course, we talked about some of it on the phone."

I hated this too. That strangers—even people like Chief Garcia and Deputy Callaway both who seemed professional and caring—were privy to private information about my life. The stalker hadn't just stripped me of my sense of safety, but my privacy too.

I cleared my throat. "I'm sure it's all there, Chief Garcia."

"Charlie, please." He smiled quickly, but it didn't seem forced.

He opened the file, one of dozens sitting on his desk. The older man obviously hadn't switched over to electronic filing. As he looked through it, he asked me a few questions, all of which I could answer almost automatically now.

Every police officer wanted to hear the story in my own words. Why, I didn't exactly know. To make sure I hadn't left anything out? To make sure I wasn't making things up? To help me tell it so many times that my brain could shut off and protect itself?

Charlie jotted down notes as I spoke and at least never made me feel like I was seeking attention with all this. Which was better than some of the early law enforcement officers I'd talked to.

"They haven't come up with an answer as to how your stalker has been locating you, correct?"

"No. I haven't been staying at my house for weeks, but he—she?—still keeps finding me."

"We'll refer to the stalker as a male for right now. That fits the profile."

"Detective Watters decided it might be best for me to stop work completely and leave the state while they try to handle things from there," I said when Charlie ran out of questions. "So, here I am in Montana. Hopefully, very short-term."

"Regardless of how long you intend to stay, I will do my best to ensure your safety. We look after our own here."

"All twenty-five hundred and eighteen of them?"

He raised an eyebrow. "Yes. And you too."

"Thanks." I wasn't ever going to be one of *theirs*, but his words soothed me just the same. He wasn't dismissing me or what had happened. That was the most important thing. "I'm going to go get my stuff moved in, if that's okay."

Charlie stood, and we walked back out into the main section of the building. "Detective Watters mentioned you were moving in to the Haven apartment complex." I nodded.

"That's a nice place," the lady who'd greeted me at the front counter said, not at all ashamed of eavesdropping.

"Maryann is right." Charlie nodded. "It's a secure location and in a safe part of town."

Now, my eyebrow rose. "Do you have a bad section in a town this size?"

Charlie smiled. "Every size town can have problems, and we've had our share. But you're right. There's not one section that's better or worse than another, for the most part."

"Except for those Resting Warrior Ranch ruffians. At least she's not on that side of town."

"The Resting Warrior Ranch Ruffians? Is that like a sports team?" I literally had no idea what we were talking about.

Charlie's belly laugh was contagious. "No, no. We have a group of former Navy SEALs who run a ranch facility just outside of town, helping people with PTSD and whatnot."

I looked between Maryann and Charlie. "That makes them ruffians?"

"Oh no," Charlie continued when Maryann rolled her eyes. "They're good guys. Although they used to be a little rowdy, which Maryann obviously hasn't forgiven. Most of them have settled down now and are married or well on their way."

"Well, I don't plan on spending much time with Navy SEALs turned ranchers, so I think we'll be okay."

"It's actually good to have them nearby. I'll be able to reach out to them for an extra layer of protection, if needed. They owe me one...or ten," he finished with a huge grin on his face. "I may share some details of the case with them, if that's okay."

I tried to force a smile onto my face. I hated the idea of having more strangers all up in my business. "Hopefully, that won't be necessary. But if it is, that's fine. Meanwhile, I'll just be lying low. Going to leave here, go straight to the apartment, and hopefully you won't hear from me again until Detective Watters lets me know it's safe to come home."

"How about if you check in each day via text or email on that burner phone of yours, so I know you're okay."

I'd already given him the info. "Sure. But beyond that, I'll be pretty scarce."

Charlie crossed his arms over his chest. "No need to stay hidden. We're a friendly bunch around here."

I shrugged. "No offense, Chief, but I'm not here to make friends. I just want to keep to myself."

Charlie and Maryann shot each other a look. No doubt it was a *city-bitch-lady alert*.

I wasn't trying to be unfriendly; I really wasn't. Hell, I worked with people day in and day out—real estate wasn't a job for a shrinking violet. I was known for being friendly.

But not now. Not here. I didn't have it in me. "I'm just here to lie low."

Charlie nodded. "Which is a smart idea. Better safe than sorry. But be careful that this place doesn't grow on you. It's been known to happen."

Not a chance. I was a city girl through and through and wasn't about to become resident 2,519.

I smiled. "I'll just stay hidden in my apartment so I'm not seduced by Garnet Bend's many charms."

Maryann shot me a smile now that I wasn't disparaging her beloved town. I waved goodbye and headed out. I really just wanted to get into my apartment and get settled. I already had the key.

I looked around before leaving the safety of the doorway, unable to walk the few feet to my car without ascertaining if threats were afoot.

Even though, I'd learned the hard way that I could look all I wanted and still not see the threat about to attack me. I had some scars to prove that.

I finally forced myself to go, gritting my teeth the whole way. Sliding in the driver's seat of my beloved Subaru eased some of the tension. I always felt safer in here.

"Okay. No more people. No more anything. Let's just get settled."

I turned the key. Nothing.

Again. And again. Nothing. *Damn it.*

"Oh, come on."

No matter how many times I tried it, the engine wouldn't turn over. I tried one final time, and with a putter and growl, it finally started.

Charlie jogged up to me, squinting as the cold breeze chilled his face. He must've been watching from the door.

I quickly rolled down the window, suppressing a shiver. "It was just struggling to start."

He cringed. "Damn. Don't know much about cars, but it may be the alternator. You'll want to get that taken care of right now. Having a drivable car is important in your situation."

"Is there anywhere in town, or do I need to go somewhere else?"

"There's a garage down the street. The new owner is a friend of the Resting Warrior Ranch guys. He's honest, and you can trust him."

I wasn't sure I felt like I could trust any stranger right now, but what choice did I have? It wasn't like I could walk around in this weather. And if I had to leave in a hurry...

"Yeah, okay. I'll give the ruffian wannabe a shot." My insides twisted at the thought, but I plastered a small smile on my face.

Charlie laughed and gave me directions to the garage, then retreated back inside the station, out of the cold.

I followed Charlie's directions, swallowing my frustration. Moving anywhere always came with hiccups. I knew that. I'd coached residential real estate clients through the headaches of relocating many times. Had done the same with commercial real estate clients from time to time too.

This was just a hiccup.

But why did it feel like an omen?

Chapter Two

Jensen

I wandered in from the repair bay of my shop to the office section, beelining for the coffeepot.

I was not the best morning person, and everybody who knew me generally tried to avoid me until after lunch or I'd drunk a full pot of coffee, whichever came first.

"Aw, come on. Empty? I've only had one cup." I narrowed my eyes at the coffeepot my office manager Susanna hadn't filled, as if my glare would cause coffee to magically appear.

Damn it.

Susanna didn't rate keeping the coffeepot filled high on her to-do list. I didn't expect her to wait on me, of course. She was here to do the books and deal with customers.

But man, actually drinking coffee rather than willing it to appear would be so much better right now.

Grumbling, I got out the needed items and started a fresh pot.

Maybe I could put up a sign threatening death to anyone who drank this batch. I glared as the machine took an excessively long time—at least fifteen seconds—to start brewing.

"Jensen?" Susanna's voice called out from the front section where she dealt with customers.

Fuck. I needed at least four more cups of coffee before talking to anyone, including Susanna.

A *people person* I was not. But coffee at least helped.

"Jensen, is that you?"

I rolled my eyes. "Who else would it be?"

I only hired a few part-timers, young guys who needed the experience. Sometimes even some of the clients staying at Resting Warrior Ranch would have an itch to get their hands dirty, just to do something while they were recovering, and I would let them tinker around with some stuff in the garage.

Business normally slowed down this time of the year anyway. It was mostly just me and Susanna unless something occurred that required more hands, and then I'd call in some part-time help.

"Come here, then," Susanna hollered from the office.

I didn't reply, crossing my arms while I waited for the coffee to drip. Not that watching it was going to make it go any faster. Still, coffee first. Susanna could wait.

"Jensen!" she hollered again.

"In a minute!" I shouted back. She was a feisty woman, just a few years younger than me. But since she'd started here, we had forged a brother-sister bickering that mostly amused me, but some-times, like now, was just annoying.

I wasn't sure what I'd do without her, though. Dealing with all the ins and outs of the business, not to mention talking all day with the customers, I'd exceed my people quota quickly each day.

As soon as my cup was brewed, I joined her in the office. While the repair bays of the garage were functional and sparse, her space in the office was an explosion of color. Knitted—crocheted? Hell if I knew the difference—scarves and blanket-things littered the coatrack and hung over the back of her chair.

"What's that?" she asked as a greeting, pointing a bright-pink pen at a box of muffins.

I almost smiled, forgetting that I'd arranged to have them delivered. "Breakfast," I replied before taking one.

"Don't you mean 'payment'?" She air-quoted the last word with the hand she wasn't using to tap that pen on the desk.

I shrugged, taking a big bite.

She furrowed her brow. "I came in to open up this morning and found them in an insulated bag at the front door."

I nodded. Mrs. Kimble had told me she'd drop them off daily this week.

"So," she continued, "I shouldn't have been surprised when I was balancing the books and discovered you'd given her a steep discount for her brake drums and rotors."

I didn't speak, just ate the muffin.

Susanna raised one thin eyebrow at me.

"Yeah," I finally forced out since I could tell she wasn't going to let it go.

"Jensen, you're giving away too many services!" She slapped her palm on the desk.

"I'm not giving away anything."

"You discounted that job by seventy percent."

She narrowed her eyes when I shrugged again.

I wasn't going to stress out Mrs. Kimble over her brakes. She was a nice older lady who owned a small house down the road. She was a longtime resident of Garnet Bend and her husband had passed away a few months ago, so she was alone except when her son and his family came for visits. She loved to cook, always providing treats for fundraisers and charity events, and her baked goods were amazing.

It would feel like taking advantage of some grandmother if I charged her full price.

"Seemed worth it," I said. "Plus, these are delicious. If you ate some, you probably wouldn't be so cranky."

I knew I was venturing out onto thin ice, but it was deliberate.

This wasn't the first time Susanna had grumbled about my method of bartering and trading, and I doubted it would be the last.

It was just the way I wanted to run things here. I didn't need the money. I lived well within my means and didn't have a lot of expenses or debt, so I could offer discounts for my services if I wanted. And bartering was my way of giving back to the community that'd taken me in and embraced me as one of their own.

"We're barely breaking even this month," she groused.

Bullshit. I cut her a look.

"Well, we are."

I tipped my chin at the computer monitor that showed all the spreadsheets I hated to ever look at. "What about the income from the extra bay?"

The Resting Warrior guys and I had added an additional bay area a year ago when we'd done the renovations. That bay wasn't for cars; it was for my woodworking. I handcrafted small wood pieces like jewelry boxes, sculptures, and animal carvings.

The guys had built it for me as a place to do what I loved the most, but it hadn't taken long for people to find out about my skills and for orders to start coming in. It was already making money.

She huffed, crossing her arms again. "Okay. With that money, we're doing fine."

Exactly. I picked up another muffin. Old Mrs. Kimble was a woman after my heart. She knew blueberry was my favorite.

"But don't you think it's a good idea to make sure the main business can stand on its own?"

"Why?" I scowled. "It's not like I'm going to stop carving stuff."

In fact, if I followed Cori's and Emma's advice—Grant's and Daniel's wives came by regularly to talk to Susanna—and put my carvings on social media and a website, I could probably get more orders. But neither Susanna nor I was good with online stuff.

I'd definitely have to find someone who could handle creating the social media and website side of my business if I were truly going to entertain those suggestions.

But I, for sure, didn't want to do it. To me, social media meant more peopling—something I tried to avoid.

"Reducing prices by seventy percent isn't a good business strategy." Susanna was twirling her pen in the air again.

"You might not feel that way if you'd try these muf—"

My phone rang, cutting off my argument. I saw Chief Garcia's name on the screen, so I answered in case there'd been a wreck or a breakdown he needed my help for.

"Just FYI, customer incoming," he told me after we greeted each other. "Her Subaru didn't want to start when she was leaving the station. It's important she doesn't get stranded, so do a full workup if you have time."

"No problem. Who is it?"

"Out-of-towner."

Interesting that the police chief was sending me a stranger who should be heading out of town soon, but business was business. "Okay. I'll look out for her."

I left Susanna to take another phone call, this one on the garage's number. She glowered at me as I turned away, letting me know she intended to pick up our argument again later.

The joy.

I took my coffee to the front window, watching for the Subaru that needed my help. Behind me, I heard Susanna talking with someone interested in buying some of my carvings. A grin pulled at my lips as she let out a slight squeak at the massive price they offered.

Small town meant a lot of word-of-mouth business. It also helped that I'd presented some pieces at recent town events so people could see my skill up close.

It took every bit of restraint not to turn around and *I-told-you-so* Susanna.

I could go pro bono with the mechanic shop if I expanded my woodwork to small furniture items. But I wouldn't. I liked things the way they were now.

The navy-blue Ascent pulled in, and I studied the vehicle. Looked pretty standard, not that I could tell all problems from a distance.

The owner parked but didn't get out, so I looked closer. And froze.

I don't know what I was expecting, but it wasn't this beautiful —and *oh-so-serious*—woman. Her brows were furrowed as if she couldn't decide whether she wanted to stay.

Her captivating pink lips mouthed the name of the garage from reading the sign before she sat back and gave an adorable pout. She flicked her dark hair over her shoulder and reached for the door handle.

I couldn't look away.

I wasn't immune to lust at first sight. Though my intimate acquaintances were not as frequent as they used to be before moving here, I wasn't a stranger to sexy women. But none of them ever caught my attention in such a way without my even talking to them. This woman was undeniably beautiful, but more than that, she was *compelling*.

Feeling this drawn to a woman at first glance had me unsettled, but the second she stepped out of her car and stood, I relaxed.

Yeah, *no thanks*.

No matter how pretty she was—and her long legs, athletic build, and slender waist just made her more so—she was not my type. She was clearly a city girl, from her business slacks down to her high heels, and I was as small-town as they came. I hadn't been raised in Garnet Bend, but small-town Iowa made me just as far out of her league.

Her long brown hair had to have been styled in a fancy salon. Her slacks and jacket were the epitome of professional business casual. She practically screamed high-maintenance.; she liked the finer things in life and probably did whatever she had to to avoid getting her hands dirty.

My hands were perpetually dirty.

She reminded me of the wealthy clients I used to work for in the security business. Appearance over substance.

The woman walked toward the front door, and I steeled myself for having to play nice.

But hopefully her engine problem could be fixed quickly. I couldn't imagine her hanging out in the plastic chairs in the waiting area for very long without throwing a fit. And there wasn't much in Garnet Bend to keep someone like her entertained.

I opened the door as she rushed in from the cold. She'd left the car running, and I heard its low growl before the door whooshed shut. That wasn't a good sound.

Then my attention was snatched away by the scent of her as she walked by, mumbling good morning. She smelled delicious. Like vanilla and apples.

Sorry, Mrs. Kimble. All the aftertaste of those blueberry muffins was gone.

"Hello. The police chief told me that you might be able to help me with my car." Her tone was light and bubbly. It was almost too chipper. It felt forced.

"Yeah. Charlie called." I held out my hand, wondering why this woman had been talking to the chief in the first place. "Jensen Chambers."

"Nice to meet you." She hesitated briefly before shaking my hand.

Evidently, princess didn't like to be touched by commoners.

"I'm Kenzie Hurst."

I ignored whatever the heck the tingle was that streaked up my arm from her touch. Bright pink-and-white manicured nails shone as she lowered her hand. Butter-soft skin. Definitely big-city.

"Pull it in, and I'll take a look." I pointed at the bay doors and proceeded to enter the garage. After I pressed the button for the garage door to open, I directed her inside the first bay. All the while, I resisted the urge to shake out my hand. Her touch lingered there.

Once she drove into the first bay and got out, she stood off to the side but kept her eyes on my every movement. I walked around, taking a closer look to see if I could figure out the problem by sight alone. Overall, everything looked well maintained.

"I hope it's nothing major," she said. "I haven't had any problems until today. I'm keeping my fingers crossed it's just a little hiccup and I can be on my way."

I nodded and stepped over to the side of the engine, which allowed me to glance into the passenger area of the car. It was full of stuff, even the front seat. "Heading on a work trip?"

"Um. Well, no." Her eyes darted around the garage as she furrowed her brow.

"Traveling for vacation?" Knowing if she planned to drive far might change the prognosis. I'd need to make sure it was roadworthy for a long drive, in that case.

"That's none of your business."

I looked over at her, raising my brows at her curt reply. Although, even terse, she was still beautiful.

Forget it, Chambers. She's not your type.

"I'm sorry. That was rude." She sighed, and it reminded me of myself before I had my coffee. "I'm just tired. This car thing is unexpected."

"I'll need to look it over and probably order some parts. May mean keeping your vehicle overnight. Do you have somewhere you can stay or someone to call?"

It was too windy outside for her to be walking, especially in the fancy shoes she had on. She definitely hadn't come prepared for the weather around here.

She stared down at the phone in her hand like she couldn't quite remember how to use it.

"I'm staying at the Haven apartment complex for a little while."

I knew the place on the other side of town. Wasn't what I was expecting, but, as she'd said, it was none of my business.

"I could take you to your place." Susanna walked over to Kenzie. She'd obviously been eavesdropping. She held up an empty coffee thermos. "I'm itching for a refill of the good stuff from Deja Brew anyway."

I rolled my eyes. Susanna wanted to gossip with her friends just as much as she wanted coffee.

"Susanna's my office manager," I told Kenzie. "She can get your information, and I can call you tomorrow with an update."

I forced myself to turn away as the women left. I needed to get the vehicle fixed and get the city beauty on her way.

Not stand here wondering why I could still feel the warmth from where I'd touched her hand.

Chapter Three

Kenzie

The next morning, I heaved a sigh and snuggled down into the soft mattress of my new bed. It wasn't the same as my normal bed, but it was comfy.

The whole place was...okay. Not bad. Just not *home*.

Susanna and I had gotten all my stuff out of my car, into hers, and then brought it over here. I'd appreciated that the other woman had helped me carry it all in. She'd wanted to stay and help me set up, but I just hadn't had the social bandwidth for it.

I didn't want to make friends here. I wasn't going to be here long enough for friends.

Plus, I didn't have enough stuff to need much help anyway. The apartment had come furnished, so all I'd needed was to put away my clothes and set up the few decorative items I couldn't live without.

I'd changed into better clothes for walking then had gone back into town for a few groceries. Not too many since I had to carry them all back.

This morning, I was thinking of my car. I wanted it back as soon as possible, even though I was within walking distance of nearly everything in Garnet Bend. I missed the comfort of knowing my car was available as a means of escape. Without it, I felt trapped here.

But if I was honest, it wasn't just my car on my mind as I lay in bed. It was Jensen Chambers.

We hadn't talked much, and, as was never far from my mind, I was not in Garnet Bend to connect with people. But...I felt a weird pull to want to know more about the handsome mechanic. He had one of those rich, deep voices, and coupled with his looks —short, dark hair, strong chin and granite cheekbones, and a body that showed very clearly he was used to hard work—I was drawn to him.

All he needed was a tool belt.

I hadn't tried to strike up small talk, and he hadn't seemed to be interested either. Actually, the fact that he barely talked to me had me more intrigued. I worked with people for a living and generally found they wanted to engage with me. But not Jensen Chambers.

I had no clue if I could count on him, despite Charlie's recommendation. His place seemed to be the only garage in town, though, so it wasn't as if I had a choice.

But the knowledge that I was going to get to talk to him soon made the thought of the long day ahead of me a little more bearable. I knew I needed to shut those feelings down, but damned if I wanted to.

My phone rang on the side table, interrupting my musings. Seeing the name of the garage flash across the screen, I extracted myself from the warmth of my covers and tried to calm the sudden dancing butterflies in my stomach.

"You're not here to make friends," I murmured into the quiet space. "Or anything else."

But it wasn't Jensen's voice on the line when I answered. It was Susanna's.

"Hey, Kenzie," she said. "Jensen says your car won't be ready today."

"Oh, okay."

"Yeah, he's waiting for some parts and wants to check out a few more things."

So it was going to be a long day sitting here in this apartment. "Thanks for letting me know."

"Hey, listen!" I stopped myself from disconnecting the call as I heard Susanna's rushed phrase. "I was hoping you would like to join me for coffee."

That was sweet. And unexpected. "Sure. I'd love to."

The words were out before I could stop them. Ah, damn it. What was I doing?

"Great! I'll swing by your place, and we can walk from there. You'll love Deja Brew."

"Yeah, sounds good. See you soon."

I hung up, excited to have something to do to fill my time today, but it soon faded to sadness.

I loved coffee dates, but I wanted the ones with my friends back in Denver. Zoe and Leah and I would call one another at the craziest hours when we needed girl time. I'd always tend to be the last one to arrive at the coffeehouse, but they knew what pick-me-up to order to make me happy when I showed up.

"Chin up," I reminded myself as I slid out of bed to get ready. "It's only temporary."

* * *

Susanna wore a bright sweater of reds and purples that meshed well with the brown puffer vest over it. On top of her head, she wore a thick brown beanie, hiding most of her auburn locks. It was a look I could never pull off. I was built for classic styles, not quirky.

"You're too cute," I said once she arrived and we set out for town.

"This?" Susanna pointed at the hat, tracing her finger over the swirled lines that gave it so much more detail. "It's nothing."

I raised a brow. "Nothing? Did you make it?"

"Sure did." Susanna beamed. "I've loved knitting for as long as I can remember. One day, I'll open my own shop."

"To sell knitted goods?"

"To sell yarn. For crafters to get supplies and make their own treasures. Maybe I can help teach them too."

I nodded. Turning a hobby into a job would be a challenge. "I wish I had a hobby like that."

"Not crafty?" Susanna guessed.

I shook my head. I'd always wanted to be. It would be so cool to have a unique thing, like making my own kombucha or creating those little crochet animals. Even cross-stitch needlework with naughty sayings. Something funky.

"But I did these myself." I held up my hands, showing Susanna my manicure I'd spent hours on while watching *Kitchen Nightmares*.

"Wow, girl. Those are so pretty! I would've sworn you had them done."

"Thanks." I smiled, admiring the reflection of them in the sunlight as we walked. "I haven't had much time to be creative, though. Since..."

I couldn't tell her about the stalker. I didn't even know the woman.

"Work?" She filled in for me when I faded off. I nodded. "Yesterday, you said you're a Realtor?"

I nodded in reply as we walked down the sidewalk. I tried to keep an eye on everyone around us without making it seem that way. I couldn't let my guard down. "I specialize in commercial real estate."

"I don't think you'll find a lot of that in these parts," Susanna mused.

"Yeah. I also teach some 'how-to' seminars, like how to branch out starting your own business, gain a customer base, dos and don'ts of commercial real estate and management. Things like that."

"That's impressive! What are you doing here in Garnet Bend?"

I should've been better prepared for that question. "I just needed a little break. Wanted to get away from everything."

Fortunately, Susanna didn't press further. She pointed out different shops and her favorite parts of town as we went.

As we got closer to the other end of the street, I could smell the delicious aromas of baked goods and coffee. Once we reached the door to Deja Brew and Susanna pushed inside, my mouth started watering from all the wonderful smells. A bright, bubbly woman with highlighted hair waved from behind the counter and motioned for us to sit.

"Is she a relative of yours?" I whispered to Susanna.

The two women were dressed so similarly, I couldn't help but ask.

Susanna turned her head to see where I was indicating and couldn't hold in a giggle. "Lena? Nah. She's the owner of Deja Brew. She's really sweet and totally cool, though."

"Hey, Sus!" Another woman with a friendly smile walked over to greet us at the table. "Escape from Jensen's horrible coffee again?"

"Girl, you know it! Jensen's coffee machine needs to be retired, but he won't part with it until it completely stops working," she replied with a huge grin. "Kenzie, this is Evelyn Everett. Evelyn, this is Kenzie Hurst."

I nodded to the delicate-looking woman in greeting.

"You want your usual and a fill-up?" Evelyn asked, glancing at Susanna's thermos.

"Please. And an apple tart too. We can come to the counter." She started to rise.

"Nah, I don't mind. We're not that busy right now. I'll bring it over." She turned to me. "What would you like?"

"It all smells so wonderful. A regular coffee and something blueberry, if you've got it."

"Great, be right back." Evelyn turned and walked back to the counter, returning with our orders a short time later. "You two enjoy. It was nice meeting you, Kenzie. Stop back by sometime soon so you can meet Lena and we can all chat."

After Evelyn walked away, we sipped our drinks and watched the town come to life through the window. Snow fell outside, making the ground look like a thick, downy blanket of white, while the residents trod along like they had all the time in the world.

It was lovely to watch, but seeing more of the white stuff falling, I was dreading the walk back to my apartment. Sure would have been nice to have my car right about now.

"Did Jensen hint at when my car might be ready?" I asked. I didn't want to nag, but I was antsy without it.

"Uh, not sure. He'll text me the minute it's done."

"So, Jensen. He's not a man of many words, is he?"

Damn it, why was I asking about him? Why couldn't I get his deep brown eyes—a warm honey color—out of my mind? Or his muscled arms?

Or the fact that I wondered if they sold tool belts anywhere in town?

"Was he rude to you? I'm sorry. He's not a morning person at all and is totally unbearable until he drinks a pot of coffee."

"No, not rude, just..." I wasn't sure how to describe it.

She rolled her eyes and dismissed me with a wave. "Jensen's bedside manner isn't the greatest—"

I choked on my sip of coffee and laughed. "Bedside manner?"

Susanna giggled too. "Sometimes it seems like he's a doctor, delivering good or bad news about people's cars."

I chuckled as I took another sip of coffee while Susanna kept talking. The other woman was good company. Sitting and chatting with her like this reminded me of my girlfriends back home.

"He's a lovable grump. I've never met a man with a bigger heart, but I swear he's got trust issues up to here." Susanna lifted her hand to indicate an imaginary height above her head.

"Hmm." Sounded just like me since the stalking started—and especially after the break-in at my home in Denver. I definitely struggled with trust issues, too.

"And Charlie said he's friends with people at a therapy ranch near here?" The ruffians had intrigued my thoughts too.

Susanna smiled wide. "Yeah. The Resting Warrior Ranch is a short drive outside of town. They help people with PTSD issues and physical therapy. They raise and train emotional support animals of all kinds. Even alpacas."

I raised my eyebrows. "Alpacas? Really?"

She grinned. "Yep. Actually, Lena and Evelyn are married to a couple of guys who run the ranch. Jude and Lucas. I'm sure you'll meet them all at some point while you're here."

I glanced at the two women working behind the counter. "Oh wow. It really is a small town."

"Everybody knows everybody, for better or worse."

More people started coming in, making it harder to talk, so Susanna and I stood to leave. "Jensen will think I quit and moved in here for the coffee if I don't get back soon."

We waved goodbye to Lena and Evelyn as we left. After coffee, we braved the snow for the walk back through town. Susanna wanted to show me the flower shop that had a sale right now on the way back, and I figured it wouldn't hurt. Maybe fresh flowers, or even a plant of some kind, would perk up my new place.

I found a plant, and we poked around a couple other shops. It was nice to get out and act like a normal person for a while. Back in Denver, it had been a while since I'd done that. Walking around outside at shops had felt like a luxury I couldn't risk.

One more thing the stalker had stolen from me.

When we got to the crosswalk, a man approached, walking directly toward us with focused purpose. I couldn't help but tense and prepare to run. I hadn't worn my good boots, but surely the shoes I had on would give me enough traction in this snow.

"Hi, Lucas," Susanna said to the man.

Okay. Susanna knew him. I tried my best to still my heart that seemed to be thundering in my chest, hating that being scared and wanting to flee were my first reactions to meeting someone who didn't mean any harm.

"Hey, Susanna. How's Jensen treating you?" Lucas greeted, nodding in my direction. He seemed nice enough, but he was huge, like a linebacker, and it made me a little uneasy.

Susanna laughed and waved her thermos around. "Oh, you know. Still having to run out for the good stuff if I want any drinkable coffee, but everything else is great." Then she turned to me. "This is Lucas Everett, Evelyn's husband. He helps run the Resting Warrior Ranch. Lucas, this is Kenzie Hurst."

I nodded, recognizing the name from our coffee shop conversation.

"Kenzie." Lucas held out his hand. Warily, I watched my small hand engulfed in his large palm. I pulled it back quickly.

"Hi, nice to meet you." I mustered a semi-smile.

If my stalker was someone of his size, I'd surely be done for.

"Uh, I'm going to head back to my place." I turned to Susanna.

"I'm eager to start unpacking. I don't want to keep you from your work any longer anyway. You can finish showing me around another time."

It was a pathetic excuse. Unpacking didn't sound fun, and I was already finished anyway, but with my nerves still bouncing around from Lucas's huge presence, I needed a little space.

I didn't want them to think I was a nutcase who couldn't handle meeting new people. Even if it was the truth right now.

Susanna waved bye and reminded me again that she'd contact me once she knew more from Jensen. I carried my little plant back to my temporary home, constantly watching for threats on my way. By the time I made it to the apartment complex, the tension had given me a headache.

I wanted to cry.

I missed my life, my friends, and my business. I thrived on the go-go-go feeling I got from meeting with clients and helping people find the perfect places to suit their needs. I loved teaching my seminars and showing people new to the business how to be successful.

I was not used to sitting around doing nothing.

I spent the entire afternoon reorganizing everything. It was mind-numbingly boring as far as tasks went, and with each thing I set out, I wondered, why bother? I didn't want to stay here.

I looked around the place. Even with my possessions in place, it still felt empty.

"Maybe I should've gotten flowers too," I mumbled. Not that that was going to help.

I took a glass of wine to the couch and decided to text Leah, then Zoe, and belatedly remembered they'd be meeting up for their weekly margaritas now. I was supposed to have as little contact with them as possible anyway.

Damn, I missed them. I moved to the next person on my list,

my mother. Texting with my mom did help a bit, but she was at work and couldn't actively chat. As a park ranger at Pawnee National Grassland, she sometimes led evening hikes.

Still bored, I decided to check on my social media business site that I used primarily for my seminars. I knew I probably shouldn't since I wasn't supposed to be doing anything business-related, but I just wanted to take a quick look.

Nothing of any consequence. My seminars for the next month had been canceled, but I still had some scheduled for this coming spring. Surely everything would be taken care of by then. I was glad to see the number of people registering was still relatively decent.

I was just about to shut everything down when I got a DM notification. I froze, not sure what to do. Open it? Delete it without opening? Maybe it was someone who had a legitimate question.

This was how it had all started. Direct messages on my social media accounts. My fingers trembled as I tapped the icon to open the stranger's message.

As soon as I did, I wished I hadn't.

> Getting out of Denver isn't far enough. Trust me.

I sucked in a breath, eyes widening, and continued to read.

> You need to leave the state, or the blood on your walls will be yours next time.

I slammed my laptop closed and jumped up from the couch, clutching my throwaway phone. I hurried to the door, then windows, checking the locks and closing the blinds. I started shaking so bad that I dropped my phone twice before making it back to the couch. Curling up in a ball, I tried to steady my breath and called the police chief.

I'd barely been in Garnet Bend for twenty-four hours, and it was starting again.

Would I ever feel safe?

Chapter Four

Jensen

I slipped out early without a word to Susanna. I knew she wondered where I'd gone at 3:30 for the past few Wednesdays, but I wasn't going to tell her. She'd just nag me about it anyway, especially after the talk we'd had yesterday about Mrs. Kimble.

I went by and got the pizza, which had become a standing order: green peppers and mushrooms with light sauce. Honestly, I was more of a meat-lovers pizza type of guy, but that didn't matter. I could eat whatever. And the pizza wasn't what this was about anyway.

Mr. Cristolman had the pizza ready for me when I walked in. I tried to pay for it, as I did every week, but he wouldn't take the money. He'd refused my payment ever since he'd figured out exactly what was happening. I hadn't planned on revealing that, but he'd seen us one day and had put two and two together because of the pizza I normally ordered versus what I ordered on Wednesdays.

"Tell Margaret I said hello."

I nodded and grabbed the box, plus the small package wrapped in foil he slid on top of it. "Thank you."

"Thank *you*, Jensen."

The admiration in the man's eyes made me uncomfortable, as it always did. All I was doing was eating a pizza.

Plus, Mrs. Kimble was good company.

A few months ago, I'd been cutting through the park in the town square when I'd spotted her eating pizza inside the tiny indoor conservatory Garnet Bend was so proud of. She'd been sitting alone inside the hexagonal greenhouse-type building that housed a ton of plants, a small water feature, and a few benches—a space open year-round, no matter the weather outdoors. Everyone in town loved it.

But Mrs. Kimble had been looking pretty sad that day, eating her pizza.

Nobody should look sad eating pizza.

I hadn't meant to go inside and ask if she was okay. I definitely hadn't meant to sit down and share a type of pizza I didn't particularly like with the older woman.

But when she explained that she and her husband Harold had had pizza there in the conservatory every Wednesday afternoon since the day it opened fifteen years ago to the day he'd died this past June, I knew I had to stay.

Green peppers and all.

Somehow it had become a Wednesday afternoon tradition for the two of us for the past few months. We ate pizza, and she talked about her Harold. She didn't seem to mind that I didn't talk much. And I didn't mind hearing stories about their fifty years of marriage.

There was rarely anyone in the conservatory on Wednesday afternoons at that time, so I was surprised when I heard voices as I opened the door.

"Oh, I smell pizza!"

That was definitely Mrs. Kimble. She said the same thing every week.

"Hi, Mrs. K."

"Jensen, come over here, hun. I have someone I want you to meet."

I made my way over to the bench in the corner where we always sat. I stopped short when I saw who was sitting next to Mrs. Kimble.

Kenzie Hurst.

At least she had more appropriate clothing on today, not high heels and dress slacks.

"Kenzie," Mrs. Kimble said, "this is my standing dinner date for Wednesday afternoons. His name is—"

"Jensen Chambers," Kenzie finished for her. "He and I met earlier this week."

I was honestly a little surprised she remembered my name. "Good to see you again."

Kenzie stood up. "I'll leave you two to your dinner. I don't want to—"

Mrs. Kimble patted the bench next to her. "Don't be silly, dear. We always have a slice or two left over. Stay here and eat with us."

She looked over at me, one eyebrow raised. I shrugged. "Is there ever any legitimate reason not to eat pizza in the middle of the afternoon on a Wednesday?"

A smile tilted those full lips. "Not that I've ever found."

Mrs. Kimble took the box and pulled out two paper plates from her bag like she always did. She handed one to each of us. "Wonderful! I'll use the box as my plate today."

Mrs. Kimble chatted as we all ate. I gave my normal grunted replies, but Kenzie was obviously better at this than I was. She asked questions to keep Mrs. Kimble talking, even turning the conversation back to the older woman when she tried to make it more about Kenzie.

I had to admit, that impressed me. I would've assumed that Kenzie was used to attention and focus on her and that she liked it that way. But even when it was logical for her to talk about herself, she kept directing the conversation back to Mrs. Kimble. It wasn't hard; all Kenzie had to do was ask about Harold, and Mrs. Kimble would happily launch into a story.

But something wasn't quite right. Now that I was closer to Kenzie, I could see that she was looking paler and a lot more tense than when she'd dropped her car off yesterday—and she hadn't been in the greatest headspace then.

Not that she was letting Mrs. Kimble know that. Again, I was impressed. Kenzie might be more big-city than small-town, but she wasn't letting a lonely widow feel anything but completely seen and heard.

I was almost through my second slice of pizza when Mrs. Kimble jumped up. "Would you look at the time? I've got to go!"

"Go do what?" I asked. She always went straight home after our meal.

"I...I forgot I had something I scheduled." She patted my arm. "Now, don't you be rude. You stay here with Kenzie and finish the pizza. I'll see you next week. I'll be sure not to...schedule anything then. Silly me."

Mrs. Kimble hugged Kenzie and fluttered out the door, despite both of us trying to get her to stay. We were both standing there just staring at each other as the door closed behind her.

"I think somebody is playing matchmaker," Kenzie finally said.

I gave her a half smile. "I'm pretty sure you're right, but we don't have to stay."

She nodded. "Yeah, don't let me keep you. I appreciate the pizza."

I recognized a dismissal when I heard one. "You're welcome. I hope to have your car ready soon."

"Thanks."

I turned to leave, but I caught her glancing at the door, almost in fear, as I did. Once again, she looked pale and tense.

Damn it.

I should just leave. It wasn't my business whether she was struggling with something or not. But somehow, I couldn't make myself move. I looked down at the small foil package Mr. Cristolman had given me. I already knew what was in it.

"Would you like a brownie?"

That shook her out of whatever had spooked her. "What?"

"The pizza place knows I have a standing dinner date with Mrs. Kimble on Wednesdays, and the owner sneaks us a treat. In her oh-so-subtle attempt to make herself scarce, I guess she forgot about them."

Kenzie raised one perfectly arched eyebrow. "Or she was trying to give you a secret weapon. Who can resist brownies?"

"Would a brownie help?"

"Help with what?"

"With whatever has that look on your face?"

She sat back down on the bench. "I don't think a brownie is going to help with that, but I'll take one anyway if you're offering."

I unwrapped the foil and offered it to her, sitting down on the bench. She began nibbling at it like she wanted to make it last as long as possible. And damned if that wasn't fucking adorable.

"How'd you end up here with Mrs. K?"

"She was here when I came by, and we started talking. We'd already been chatting a couple hours when you got here."

"She's a nice lady."

Kenzie studied her brownie like she was trying to decide which part to eat next. "Very nice. Misses her husband very much. I enjoyed talking to her, and I was glad she was here."

They'd talked for two hours? I had misjudged Kenzie. "How'd you end up here in the conservatory?"

"I had an...issue, and I had to go see Charlie. I'm sure you know him, right? The police chief?" She took another tiny bite. "Of course you do. He sent me over to you about the car."

"Yes. And also, pretty much everyone knows each other here." Another nibble. "Small town."

"That's right. I assume you're not from a small town?"

"Denver. Much bigger."

I grunted in agreement. She took another little bite.

"Is everything okay? Did Charlie get you what you need?"

"Yes and no. Charlie reminded me of why I'm in Garnet Bend."

I had to admit, I would love to know more about that. Not only out of sheer curiosity but because I'd like to know more about Kenzie herself. She obviously wasn't the self-absorbed person I'd pegged her as yesterday. Not if she'd spent the afternoon talking to Mrs. Kimble.

But I also understood not wanting to have someone all up in your business when you didn't really know them. So, I decided not to push for details. I took a much bigger bite of my own brownie.

"You're not going to ask why I'm here?"

"I figure it's none of my business unless you want to tell me."

She narrowed her eyes at me. "What would be your guess?"

I leaned back against the bench. "My first guess would've been something to do with professional burnout. But since Charlie sent you to me with the car, and then you saw him again today, I'll assume it's something a little more than that."

She nodded. "I'm impressed. You're observant."

"I've never been much of a talker, but I do try to take in details of what's going on around me."

She took a bigger bite of her brownie. "I ran into a...little trouble back in Colorado."

"Someone trying to hurt you?" That did not sit well with me. At all.

"How do you know I wasn't the one causing the trouble?"

"Not to sound all supersleuth, but I assume you wouldn't have gone to our police chief twice if you were the big lawbreaker." I finished the last bite of my brownie. "Do you want to talk about your trouble?"

"Not really. I just want it to be over and get back to my regular life. I'm here so that can hopefully happen."

"Well, I'll try to make sure your car is ready for you for when it does."

She popped the rest of the brownie into her mouth and stood up. "Thank you. For dinner. For the brownie."

"Thank you for the company."

She gave me a small smile and walked toward the door, turning right before she opened it. "Do you really eat here with Mrs. Kimble every week?"

I shrugged. "As often as I can. We both like it."

She nodded. "Charlie reminded me today that I'm safe here, even though I may not feel like it all the time. Knowing that there are people like you here who take care of people like Mrs. Kimble? That helps me believe that what Charlie said was true."

She was out the door without another word, leaving me with more questions than answers.

Chapter Five

Jensen

I closed the bay doors, grabbed my duffel bag, and headed toward the office. I needed to get the hell out of here.

Susanna's voice had me stopping short of the door. "Hey, Jensen."

I paused, hoping she wouldn't try to keep me for long. I was going out to Resting Warrior to meet Lucas and Liam for a workout in their gym.

"Do we have an update on Kenzie's car? I told her I'd keep her in the loop."

I grimaced. Kenzie's car was what had me ready to put my fist through a wall. So, I was on my way out to Resting Warrior.

Something was very fucking wrong. It was one more reason I looked forward to seeing the guys. I needed to get their advice.

I shook my head. "Not yet. I'll tell you when it is."

Susanna frowned but nodded. "Okay. See ya, boss."

Driving out to the ranch was one of the things I enjoyed most about being here. Montana, in general, was great, surrounded by mountains and all the open beauty of the land. But there was something even more impressive about Resting Warrior Ranch.

Lucas and the guys had created something special and lasting with that place. Not just because of the mountains and scenery, which was beautiful enough, but because of what they did there. Helping people.

Plus, they had found the loves of their lives and were happier than I'd ever seen any of them in all the years I'd known them. I couldn't help but be a tad envious of that part.

The huge gate was open when I arrived. I saw a few of the wives outside as I drove around to the gym in back of the main lodge.

"Ladies!" I called out through my open window, and they all waved in return.

At the gym, I saw that Lucas had already started his reps with dumbbells. Liam was still warming up, stretching, getting ready for some deadlifting.

"Hey, brother. Glad you could finally make it. It's been a while." Lucas greeted me between reps as I walked in the door.

"Yeah, been getting some extra orders for my wood carvings. I've been staying pretty busy."

"Good to see you, Jensen," Liam called out as he moved to the bench to wrap his hands.

I wondered if I should just start right off with telling them about Kenzie's car, but then I changed my mind. I was wound tight and needed to release some stress. Once we were finished and cooling down, I'd bring it up and get their thoughts on it.

For the next hour, the guys took turns with the bags and in the ring. It'd been a while since I had worked my muscles like that, but it was a good feeling.

Beating the shit out of something—even a canvas bag—alleviated stress in a way nothing else quite could. By the time we were done, I felt more centered.

"So, what's on your mind?" Lucas tossed me a bottle of water then collapsed on the mat.

He'd always been able to read me. "Why do you ask that?"

He quirked a brow and unwrapped his hands. "I can tell something's going on."

"Okay, fine. I wanted to run something by you guys and get your opinion." I drank the full bottle of water, then sat down on the bench. "It's about a car that a customer brought in a few days ago. Charlie sent her over when her car wouldn't start at the station."

"She new in town or passing through?" Lucas asked out of the blue.

"That's an odd question. But yeah, she said she's staying for a bit. Why?"

"Is her name Kenzie?" Lucas moved back to recline against the wall, facing both Liam and me. "I met a woman in town with Susanna a couple days ago, and she seemed a little jumpy. Made an excuse to leave pretty quickly after I walked up."

Liam snorted. "Probably freaked out by your size."

Lucas frowned and tossed his sweaty towel at him. We all knew Lucas's own wife had once been frightened by his size.

"Yeah, Kenzie Hurst. That's her." I nodded. "I looked her car over briefly when she arrived at the garage. She'd been having trouble getting it to start."

"Could you fix it?" Liam asked.

"Spark plugs, so yeah. Should've been a twenty-dollar fix. But something else was bugging me, and I started digging around more. I found some disturbing things."

Both the guys stiffened at my words, and it felt like the air in the room went still.

Lucas rose to his feet and gave me a serious look. "Define disturbing."

I didn't like this. Didn't even like to say it.

"Her car looks like it's been tampered with. A smorgasbord of fuckery."

"What?" Lucas asked. "Are you sure?"

"Hell yes, I'm sure. Her lug nuts had been loosened. Two were missing. Her fuel was watered down. The fuel gauge was tampered with. And something's wrong with her electrical system, but I haven't completely figured that out yet. I can tell it's affected the alternator, but it's messed up the brake system too. I'm actually surprised she made it here in one piece."

Lucas cursed under his breath at the same time as Liam whistled through his teeth.

"So, I'm not sure how to proceed. She mentioned that she'd had some trouble and that's why she's in Garnet Bend. Do I bring her in and tell her what I found, or just tell Charlie and let him take over? He's the one who sent her to the garage in the first place."

"Any way this is all a coincidence?" Lucas asked.

I shook my head. "No. Somebody was deliberately trying to fuck with her. To what end, I have no idea."

I could still see her face in my mind from yesterday afternoon—features pale and pinched. She was already scared. Hearing about her car was going to make it much worse.

"Brother, that's a tough call. But since Charlie sent her, I'd go to him first and see how he wants to handle it," Lucas replied, nodding as he spoke.

Liam walked over and slapped me on the back. "Yep, I agree with Lucas. If Charlie sent her, then she had to be at the police station for a specific reason. Maybe that has something to do with what you found. I'd definitely let him make the call."

"That's where my thoughts were going too. It'd be better coming from him anyway." I retrieved my phone from my bag and stepped away to make the call. But something wasn't sitting right with me.

"Invite him to come out here, and we'll see if we can do anything to help," Lucas called out before the door closed behind me.

There. *That* felt more right.

* * *

I heard the police cruiser pull up just after Lucas, Liam, and I made it into the great room—high, vaulted ceilings with a huge fireplace and leather couch. Daniel, the unofficial leader of the Resting Warrior team, joined us. If there was something going on, he wanted to know about it.

Daniel answered the door at the knock, but it wasn't Charlie he led inside, it was Charlie's top deputy, Lachlan Callaway. I liked the man. He had a good head on his shoulders and Charlie depended on him for a lot. In a few years when Charlie finally retired, no one doubted Lachlan would be taking over as chief.

"Evening, fellas. Charlie was feeling a little under the weather so Linda made him come home. Blood pressure stuff." We all nodded in return and walked farther into the room. None of us liked thinking about Charlie's heart issues, but the man was getting up there in age.

"Jensen, thanks for the call," Lachlan continued. "Charlie has gotten me up to speed with Kenzie Hurst's case. I'm glad you suggested meeting here, because this sounds like something we might need help with."

"Sure," Lucas replied. "You know we'll help if there's anything we can do."

"But I'd like for us to try to keep the contact to this place minimal." Daniel frowned in Lachlan's direction. "It's been quiet here for a while now. We don't need to bring more trouble to our door."

All the men nodded. It wasn't just them here anymore. The women they loved were a factor as well. They wouldn't put them in danger.

"We've definitely had enough trouble to last a long while." Liam plopped down on the leather sofa.

"Of course. I don't want to see any more trouble for you guys either." Lachlan glanced around the room at each of the men.

"So, how can we help?" Daniel asked.

"Well, first, Kenzie gave us permission to share specifics of her case with you, but she didn't necessarily like it."

Specifics of her case. That meant there was some real trouble going on here. I wanted to know what it was. I couldn't stop thinking of how worried she'd been yesterday.

"Here're the basics," Lachlan began. "Kenzie is a highly successful commercial real estate guru in Denver."

I wasn't surprised to hear any of that. It was basically how I'd pegged her as soon as she'd gotten out of her car.

"She's been dealing with a stalker. Recently, it escalated into something pretty ugly."

The more Lachlan talked, the more my gut tightened. A fucking *stalker*. One that had forced her to leave her home.

"It started online through social media. Vague threats that could've come from any troll with some sort of a grudge. But then it grew into the stalker physically following her, violence against her, and defiling her home."

I started pacing back and forth. There was nothing I wanted to do more than put my fist through a wall, and I didn't even have details.

"After the last event, the Denver detective on the case suggested our town as a good place to lie low since he knew Charlie and of you guys from their conversations. Knew we'd watch out for anything suspicious." He looked over at me. "I'd say what you found is definitely suspicious."

"I'd say so too."

"Especially after we got a call from Kenzie in a panic the other night," Lachlan continued.

Hearing those words, I felt my whole body tense. I tried to quickly relax my muscles so none of the guys would notice, but

Daniel and Lucas both raised an eyebrow in question. I ignored them and rolled my shoulders, then turned my attention back to Lachlan.

"She got on one of her social media accounts and was sent a message while she was on. It was a threat, and she called the station immediately."

"It sounds like this all started as a social media troll. Maybe someone not happy with her business?" Lucas volunteered.

Lachlan nodded in agreement. "She also teaches how-to seminars for real estate newbies. Someone could have been unhappy with a class or the way she approached a certain subject."

"But it's definitely someone who keeps up-to-date with her online activity. They were waiting for her to get on and then sent the message. They probably have a program that lets them know anytime she's live on social media," Liam said.

"What did the message say?" I asked.

Lachlan pulled out a little notepad. "Getting out of Denver isn't far enough. Trust me. You need to leave the state, or the blood on your walls will be yours next time."

The mention of spilling Kenzie's blood had me wanting to punch walls again. But the phrasing was interesting. "The stalker doesn't know where she is if they're telling her to get out of the state. She's already out of Colorado."

Lachlan nodded. "That's what ultimately reassured Kenzie, I think. At least enough to keep her from freaking out completely. The stalker thinks she's closer to home."

But she'd still been alone and terrified. I clenched my fingers into fists again.

"The stalker knows she's not in Denver anymore, which isn't surprising, given the escalation," Lachlan said. "They were probably trying to get her to slip up online and give information about her whereabouts."

"Does the Denver detective have any leads yet?" Liam asked from the sofa.

"Nothing new. I filled him in on the recent events before I came here. What about what you found, Jensen?"

I shook my head. "Whoever has her in their sights isn't playing around."

I didn't know Kenzie at all, but the thought of what had been done to her car...the sort of danger she'd been in without even being aware of it? I shouldn't care, but I did.

"What was done to her car could've been deadly," I continued. "At best, she might have gotten stranded. But if the weather had taken a turn for the worse and she'd done much more driving, it could've easily forced her off the road violently—impossible to recover from. In my opinion, someone was trying to kill her."

"Fuck." Liam was the one who muttered it, but it captured what all of us were feeling.

"All of this needs to be investigated further, and we need your help keeping an eye on Kenzie," Lachlan said. "We don't have the staff. I know you guys don't know her, but Charlie said to tell you he'd take it as a personal favor."

"For Charlie, we're on it," Daniel volunteered, and the other men nodded.

Relief flooded my system at Daniel's words. There was no way I could keep an eye on Kenzie all by myself, plus run the garage. Not that it was my responsibility to keep her safe, but I knew I wasn't going to abandon her to deal with whoever this stalker was herself.

Neither were the rest of the Resting Warrior Ranch guys. This was what they did.

What *we* did.

"We'll dig around with our sources and then fill you in if we find anything," Daniel continued. "Then you guys can fill in the Denver detective as needed. Does that work for everyone?"

"Agreed," the guys all called out in unison.

The next hour was spent coming up with a plan to help Kenzie that would still allow us all to handle our normal daily duties here and in town. Daniel got the other Resting Warrior guys on speakerphone and filled them in.

Not a single one said they couldn't help. None of them even asked for more info about Kenzie. They just knew one of their own was making a request, and that was enough.

"Can you look into the identity of the person who's been DMing Kenzie threats?" Daniel asked Jude. On the Resting Warrior team, he had the most skill with computers.

"Sure, I've got some backdoor ways I can dig around. See what pops up," Jude offered.

"I can help with that too," Harlan volunteered.

I crossed my arms. "Sucks that the Denver PD is taking so long to investigate."

"I doubt they're being slow on purpose," Lachlan said. "Watters is a good man. But we do have less crime here. And with you guys helping, we have more resources to expend."

"That's true," Lucas agreed.

And it was. Hell, law enforcement aside, among the eight of them, we wouldn't have any problem handling Kenzie's safety, while the police handled the town and served as backup.

"Hey, what about Cole?" Liam chimed in. "We could use his skills."

Daniel was already shaking his head before Liam finished talking. "He and Rayne aren't back yet. Her conference lasts through the weekend, at least."

"He'd be a good asset to have if we get stuck," Noah pointed out. Cole had ties with the FBI.

The others nodded in agreement, and Daniel added, "Yeah, if we can't figure this out before they get back, we'll read him in when they return and see what he thinks."

"Okay. It seems like you've got everything covered for now, and I can't thank you enough for your help." Lachlan stood. "I know this will be a weight off Charlie's shoulders.

Everyone nodded. If they could take one small thing off the older man's list, especially after all he'd done for them over the years, that was the least they could do. "I'll leave you guys to it and head back to town."

Daniel and Lachlan started walking to the door when Lachlan suddenly stopped and turned back to me. "One last thing. If you wouldn't mind sharing your news with Kenzie about her car? It would probably be better coming from the mechanic in case she has questions. Let her know you've informed us, and Charlie will check in with her later."

"Sure. No problem," I agreed. I tamped down my excitement at the thought of seeing her again and turned back to the others and the planning while Daniel escorted Lachlan out.

"Jenson, I think you should serve as point bodyguard for Kenzie, if you don't mind," Daniel said when he came back in.

"Me?" I wanted it, but I wasn't sure I was the best choice.

"You've got the security background, and you're closest. And… I think you're the most invested."

There was that silence again, but now everyone looked at me with a variety of expressions, from raised eyebrows, smirks, and Liam's boisterous laugh. They knew I was attracted to her, but no one wanted to call me on it right now.

"You," Lucas confirmed, as if it wasn't already obvious.

"Yeah, okay. I can do it."

I was much better building or fixing stuff with my hands than I was people, but I couldn't say no. Didn't want to say no. Yes, I was attracted to Kenzie, but there was something else, something more. I couldn't explain it, but I had a need in my gut to make sure she was safe.

"But are you sure?" Daniel questioned. "We know you're not

big on having people in your personal space, so if it's a problem, we'll figure something else out."

"I'm sure. You guys all have your hands full here. Plus, you have wives and families. I'll take point."

"He's interested," Liam added with a huge grin. "Why don't you ask her out? Two birds, one stone and all that."

"I don't see that happening. We're too different," I replied. "Plus, you know me. I don't date."

Relationships had never been my forte. Not as a kid when I'd gotten bounced around from foster family to foster family and not as an adult.

Loving a woman wasn't on my radar. Not today and not tomorrow. I wasn't at that place in my life right now. Probably never would be.

And Kenzie wasn't my type anyway.

Maybe if I repeated that enough in my mind, it would sink in once and for all.

Chapter Six

Kenzie

This apartment was about to drive me crazy. Chief Garcia had called me again this morning to reassure me multiple people were working on my case and that despite the other night's message, I was still safe here.

I agreed with what he said about the wording of the message. The stalker thought I was still in Colorado, even if not in Denver.

So, safe? Yes.

Bored out of my mind? Definitely yes.

I had no work, no friends, no car. I could only read, watch TV, or do yoga for so many hours in one day. My phone dinged, and I rushed over to grab it. Hell, even a message from the stalker would be something.

But even better, it was a text from my friend Leah.

Missing you something fierce today. I wanna talk shop. Got some properties I could use your opinion on. Can't talk now, but text me your thoughts.

Send me the links.

I was desperate for some connection to my friends. Leah and

Zoe were also both in real estate, and we all loved chatting properties and talking shop when we had the chance. I had met both
women through my seminars early on in my career, and they were
like the sisters I'd never had.

We'd been there for one another through tons of stuff. Zoe's
divorce. Leah's parents' deaths. My ex-boyfriend Alan losing his
shit when my career picked up and his didn't. He'd even gotten
violent.

Alan had been the first person I suspected when this stalker
situation started, but he was still in jail from when I'd had him
arrested.

Seeing Leah's pics and specs online wouldn't be the same as
seeing the real property and talking it out with her, but at least it
was something to do. I pulled out my laptop and looked at what
Leah sent.

Doing this just made me miss my life and my friends more. I
wanted to see Leah in person, to hear her laugh, to tell her about
what a hottie Jensen Chambers was. Chatting through text or
online just wasn't the same as getting a drink with her and Zoe.

As an only child, I had always wished for siblings, and they
were the closest I'd ever found.

Trying to shake off my melancholy, I scrolled through the
information on my laptop. I could see why she was excited about
the property, but I also saw some potential pitfalls too. I texted
my thoughts back to her on my burner phone since I wasn't
supposed to send any emails in case they could be tracked by the
stalker.

Even once that was done, I still wasn't feeling brave enough to
check into my social media accounts after last night's message. I
wouldn't avoid social media forever, but Charlie had advised that
avoiding it altogether might be best for my mental health
right now.

A little step back, he'd called it, and it was sweet how considerate he was of my stability, not just concerned for my safety in his town.

I got a daily check-in message on the temporary phone from my dad and smiled. He taught mathematics at a community college, and he and my mom couldn't have been more opposite. She was outdoorsy and athletic, and he was the palest, computer-nerd man, almost like a vampire staying behind his screens and always indoors.

I read through his latest "jokes" and even chuckled at them. Dad jokes were one thing, but coupled with his math nerd humor, it was puns galore.

I missed him too, and my mom, but they both supported my decision to lay low out of town. Even if they didn't like it.

My phone buzzed again, but this time, it was a call.

Unknown number.

I couldn't help it—my breathing came in quicker pants, and my heartbeat pounded hard against my chest. Detective Watters had cautioned me not to pick up a call from anyone I didn't know, but that had been on my regular phone. I didn't know if that applied to this one too.

Although a phone call couldn't be worse than the stalker nearly running me down in a parking lot or trashing my house and painting the walls with animal blood, right?

But yet, it somehow felt more personal. I flinched as the ringtone stopped, and I stared at the phone where it sat on the couch cushion.

Would they call again?

Leave a nasty voice mail?

How'd they get my number?

Could they use it to track down where I was?

Was I safe here?

What if—

I sucked in a harsh breath when the phone chirped, signaling a text. I blinked, trying to breathe steadily through my climbing anxiety as I picked it up.

> Hey, it's Jensen, from the garage. I just tried to call, but maybe texting is better. I'd like to update you about your car.

I closed my eyes, sagging down into the couch. Jensen. Not the stalker.

Another text popped up.

> The problem is more complicated than I first thought. I'd like to know if I could pick you up and bring you to the garage to explain.

Pick me up? I wished the circumstances were different. Like he was coming to get me for a date. Even a booty call.

Laughing out loud, I chided myself. A date? *A booty call?* I was obviously struggling to keep it together more than I'd thought.

But still. Jensen Chambers was no hardship on the eyes. That sexy voice of his was no problem either.

It was still surreal to even be attracted to him, but there was no denying the fact that I was. I forced an image of him shirtless with a tool belt right out of my mind.

> Okay. That's acceptable.

I hit send then immediately regretted it. "Ugh. That's too formal. What's wrong with me?"

I quickly added,

> Thank you! 😃

Shit. The smiley emoji was probably too much in the other direction. But to send anything else would just make it worse. I set the phone down on the table before I got any other bright ideas.

He responded back with a time, and I went to get ready. It was still so chilly outside that I didn't want to switch out of my jeans and furry boots, but I changed tops to a soft sweater and spent a little extra time on fixing my makeup. Maybe he wouldn't be able to notice how tired my eyes looked now.

As if that's what I should be worrying about.

I fought back a groan when I met Jensen downstairs and got in his truck with him. He smelled so damn good, it was almost overwhelming. Like the fresh outdoors and just a hint of diesel. Both were manly, rugged scents that weren't part of my daily life, but that only added to the appeal. I had to fight the urge to inhale.

No sniffing.

Don't sniff.

Do. Not. Sniff!

I squirmed slightly in the seat and cleared my throat, unnerved by how much his presence affected me. It had to be the stress of this whole situation.

"So." The word was out before I could stop it.

God, that was worse than silence since I didn't have anything to add to it.

"So," he repeated.

"It's been pretty cold lately, huh?"

The weather? It was like I'd never had a conversation before. Me, who spent day in and day out with people and literally taught classes on how to make other people feel comfortable as a real estate agent.

"Uh, yeah. Cold. Montana gets pretty cold."

"Denver does too." I chewed on my bottom lip, trying to think of something else to say. "Um. Looking forward to the spring?"

He glanced over at me like he was trying to figure out if I was having a breakdown. Not too far off.

Finally, he replied. "Sure."

"Yeah, I am too. It's always nice to see everything green and blooming again."

He grunted.

Damn it. This was getting worse by the minute. Thank God we didn't have far to go.

"Have you always wanted to be a mechanic?"

As soon as the question was out, I mentally cringed. That was the equivalent of asking what someone's major was in college.

"Not really."

Hmm. Okay, that was interesting. But he didn't elaborate. Now what?

"I wasn't sure I'd like real estate, but it's definitely my calling."

"Mm-hmm."

"I love seeing people discover what they need. It feels so good to help someone find their place."

Another grunt.

Oh hell. I was done. He obviously didn't want to talk. Clearly, the only attraction at play here was one-sided. I turned my head to look out the window instead.

Once I scanned the scenery, I frowned. Wait. I didn't recognize any of it. Not at all. I'd only been in Garnet Bend for a couple of days, but this didn't look like the reverse of the route Susanna took when she brought me to the apartment from the garage.

Where was he taking me? My adrenaline suddenly skyrocketed, and I casually reached my hand toward the door handle. Open fields spread as far as I could see, not small-town streets. The garage was at the end of town, but this looked too rural. I should have been paying attention instead of trying to make conversation.

"See that house up over there?" Jensen asked in his deep voice. It jarred me from my panic.

"What about it?" I licked my lips, proud that my anxiety didn't reflect in my voice.

"There's a cabin beyond it. I've been fixing it up in my spare time. Aside from the garage, I also do woodcarvings and have been getting into light carpentry, thanks to my friends at Resting Warrior. Hopefully someday in the near future, I'll have it fixed up."

I exhaled a long breath. "That sounds nice."

"I took the long way around town so I could show it to you. I don't want you to think I'm about to kidnap you or something."

I laughed, trying my best to make it light, but I had no clue if I succeeded. He could have no idea how close to the truth his statement was. I hated that I was paranoid all the time, that I automatically distrusted.

"I'd love to see some of your woodcarvings sometime," I finally said.

He nodded. "I'd like to show them to you."

I glanced at him with a small smile. "So, Resting Warrior. Both Susanna and Chief Garcia mentioned it to me. The owners are friends of yours?"

"Lucas and I go way back—he's like a brother to me. After high school, he went into the Navy and worked his ass off to become a SEAL, and I went into private security."

Private security. Interesting. "How'd you end up as a mechanic?"

"The right opportunity came around about a year ago. I'd always been good with engines. Good with anything with my hands."

I glanced at his big hands on the steering wheel. Manly hands —strong and callused from hard work.

They were sexy. I had no doubt he was good with them in *all* ways.

If I said that out loud, I was going to shoot myself.

"And you like being a mechanic?"

"Yeah. Although the woodworking keeps me busier these days. But mostly, I like being here near Resting Warrior. Supporting something important."

I wanted to ask more questions, but we pulled up at the garage. Jensen led me straight to my car.

"You said it's complicated," I reminded him, feeling the need to brace myself. But for what, I wasn't yet sure.

He nodded. The troubled look on his face bothered me, like maybe I wasn't ever getting my car back again.

"So, what are we talking about? A longer wait for parts or a longer time to fix everything?" Nervousness made my words come out too rapidly. "I'll be here for a little while, so I can be patient."

He shook his head. "I wish that was it. I am, in fact, waiting on a couple things, but that's not the real problem."

"Okay, hit me with it."

He let out a sigh. "Look, I want you to know that I talked to Charlie yesterday. Actually, he came out and talked to the whole Resting Warrior team. He told us about your stalker."

Damn it. I really hadn't wanted Charlie to do that. "Why? Because of the social media message a few nights ago? It wasn't necessary for him to go running to you guys."

"He didn't come running to us. I called him."

I didn't understand. "Why?"

"Because when I was fixing your car, I found significant evidence that someone had tampered with your vehicle."

My anger disappeared, and ice started to form in my belly. I rubbed at it with my fist to try to ease the ache there. "Tampered?"

"Watered down your fuel, messed with the fuel gauge so it wouldn't register when your tank was low, loosened lug nuts on your tires—you would've eventually lost one, probably mid-drive. If that happened on a highway, it could be incredibly dangerous. Messed with your brakes."

"The stalker."

He nodded. "Definitely someone who was trying to hurt you. Probably more, to be honest."

I kept staring at my car. I couldn't even seem to make sense of his words. "What are you saying?"

"What was done to that vehicle was meant to cause serious damage. Run you off the road, maybe even kill you."

I rubbed my eyes. I'd known the stalker wanted to hurt me, had scars on my knees to prove it. But this felt so much more immediate.

"The stalker is getting more dangerous," I finally whispered.

"It seems that way." Jensen nodded solemnly. "I'm sorry. Honestly, you're lucky you made it here in one piece. I can think of half a dozen ways this combination of tampering could've been deadly."

I shook my head, panic starting to hum along my skin. I'd been close to possibly dying and hadn't even known it. Thought I was escaping toward safety, when really, I'd been heading into more danger.

"If it hadn't been for your spark plugs going bad and causing your car not to start—a completely unrelated issue, by the way— nobody would've ever caught this. You would've just been driving one day soon, and catastrophe would've hit."

I wrapped my arms around myself, trying to tamp down the panic.

"Hey." He stepped closer.

I didn't know what to do or say. I was probably overreacting, but I couldn't help it.

The stalker had taken yet another piece of my life when I'd thought I was safe. First my house, and now my car. He was with me everywhere. I couldn't escape him. No matter what I did.

My vision blurred, and my chest tightened to the point where I couldn't breathe.

"Kenzie?"

I heard Jensen's voice almost at a distance through the roar of panic in my head. I wanted to respond, but I couldn't seem to force myself to do so. I felt like I was going to shake apart.

Jensen ran his hand up my arm. "Hey, City. Stay with me, okay? It's going to be all right."

The smell of him got through to me in a way his words couldn't. That spicy, clean scent I'd already come to recognize as his. It was a tiny thread of something familiar, and my mind latched on.

I couldn't stop myself; I stepped closer. He gently pulled me into his arms. Almost immediately, I felt calmer. Safer. Maybe I didn't quite relax, but the panic receded.

"You're not in this alone," he whispered. "We're going to help you figure this out."

I nodded at his words, rubbing my cheek against his shirt. I gripped the cotton tighter in my fist, reveling in the soothing timbre of his voice and the strength of his touch.

I could only pray what he was saying was the truth.

Chapter Seven

Jensen

Kenzie was only a couple of steps away from having a breakdown. I'd never had a stalker, but I could remember the feeling of panic wash over me as a kid.

There'd been so much I couldn't control then: my addict parents and how they would behave. Then once I was in foster care, I'd never known how long any given family would want or have room for me.

Feeling like you weren't in control of your life was pretty fucking scary. So, if Kenzie needed me to hold her for a little bit while she figured out how to put herself back together, I would damn well do that.

Not that it was any hardship to hold this petite beauty with her big personality. Hell, I'd driven all the way around the opposite side of town just to have a few minutes of talking with her before coming here. I'd probably scared her to death. When I'd made that joke about not kidnapping her, she'd laughed a little too brightly.

And I had no idea why I'd felt the need to talk to her about the cabin I was fixing up. That wasn't something I generally brought up with anyone, even though it was some of my best woodwork-ing. But somehow, I wanted Kenzie to know about it.

That didn't make any sense at all. Hell, none of my behavior when it came to this woman did.

"Charlie told us some of the facts of the case, but do you want to talk about it?" I finally asked. Talking about it at least got stuff out in the open where it didn't have to feel like it was suffocating you. I knew that for a fact, too. Although I wasn't very good at following my own advice sometimes.

She nodded, pulling away a little so she could see my face. I hated seeing the sadness that lingered in her dark-brown eyes. A turbulent storm shone in their depths, and all I wanted to do was make it disappear. I wished she didn't have to deal with any of this.

"I'm sure you have to be thinking I'm overreacting." She stepped back completely out of my hold.

I found myself wanting to pull her back in, but I stuffed my hands in my pockets instead. "I don't. Not at all. I promise."

"I just want this to be over." She wrapped her arms around herself like she was trying to keep herself together.

I moved over to her side, staying close but not touching. "It will be. I'm sure of it."

She stared out in front of her. "This past July, I posted about an upcoming series of seminars I was hosting. Different aspects of commercial real estate. I've done these for a while now, and they've always been pretty popular. Gives people a chance to know what to expect in the business."

I wasn't surprised to hear her seminars were popular. Kenzie was obviously friendly and engaging. People would respond to that. "I'm sure you sell out your classes."

She shrugged. "They're generally pretty full. But for some reason, this summer, my seminar posts kept getting flooded with vicious comments on social media sites. At first, my friends and I thought they were bots attacking the classes."

"But they weren't?"

"No, bots are usually fake posts trying to get people to click on fake links. These posts were personal attacks against me."

I didn't fucking like that. Involuntarily, one of my hands clenched into a fist. "In what way?"

She shrugged again. "You know, the usual cyber abuse—commenting on stuff like my clothes, my hair, my weight, my gender."

"What the hell?"

"How I should shut up and stop talking about things I don't really understand," she continued. "The comments upset me, but I'd dealt with them before. It comes with the territory of having a bigger following. As more people became aware of my online presence and posts, the creepers, particularly men, commented and sent me DMs."

My eyes narrowed. "What did you do?"

"Mostly ignored them. It's a male-dominated industry, and there are always guys who get butthurt over a woman breaking into their good ol' boys' network." She shot me a side glance. "No offense."

I rolled my eyes. "Any man who's threatened by a woman's legitimate success is not much of a man at all."

She gave me a short nod of respect.

"In August, the messages became more abusive online, but they seemed to come from the same source. I told myself it was just the fuddy-duddy, disgruntled agents I'd dealt with before or ex-coworkers from previous employments. I had phone calls to my office line where they'd hang up. Annoying, but nothing too bad."

"But then it escalated." She wouldn't be hiding out here in Garnet Bend otherwise.

"Yes. I think someone tried to run me off the road, but I had no proof. My office was vandalized."

I narrowed my eyes. "The cops did nothing?"

She shook her head. "Not at first. They said nothing could link the events together. Said the driver might have been drunk. The vandalism wasn't necessarily related to any stalking since other vandalism had happened recently in the area."

She pulled out her phone and scrolled through pictures. I scowled when she handed it to me. A photo of her showed X marks over her eyes. The next picture showed a typewritten letter that read ***You're not welcome here. Get out.***

"Fucker," I breathed. I thought I said it under my breath, but she must have heard because she nodded in agreement.

"I got that in my mailbox in September. And in October, I was walking to my car one evening after work, and someone shoved me from behind. I was knocked to the ground. Whoever it was disappeared before I could get a look at them."

"Were you hurt?" I asked.

She swallowed hard. I knew this was hard for her to talk about —not that anyone would blame her for that. "Bloody knees, skinned hands. Nothing awful."

"But still damned scary."

"Yeah. And frustrating. I don't want to say that the police weren't helpful, but it sure felt that way. They kept saying the incidents were isolated, so they couldn't really do much."

"That's a shit-ton of stuff to be isolated."

She let out a sigh. "I'll never forget an officer explaining that sometimes bad luck just happened. And that just because it did, it didn't mean someone was after me."

"This was definitely more than bad luck."

"Finally, later in the month, I came home and found my house door ajar. The whole place was trashed." Kenzie cleared her throat. "The words GET OUT were painted across the walls in blood. I'll never forget that."

Blood? I couldn't believe what I was hearing. That was some next-level shit. "That had to have been terrifying."

"I found out it was animal blood, but still..." Her lower lip trembled.

I edged closer, fighting the urge to put my arm around her. She slid toward me, though, leaning into my side.

That felt good. *Right*. I didn't want to think about it too deeply, just wanted to lend my support.

"I went back to the police, and they still dismissed me. Said it was a Halloween prank. But my mom and dad told me to go to another station. My friends came with me, adamant that someone listen, and that's when we were put in touch with Detective Watters. He looked at it all as a whole and agreed I was definitely in danger."

"Finally."

"I couldn't go back to my place, but he advised me to lie low elsewhere. I floated between my friends' houses and my parents', but that was risky too. I didn't want my friends or family to be targeted, so I switched to hotels and bounced around, trying to stay under the radar. And messages were coming nearly every day. Every single time I got on my computer, I had emails and messages from the stalker."

The tremor in her voice and dejected slump of her shoulders told me how much this was costing her. She was on the verge of tears.

All I could think of was that I wanted to protect her. To do whatever she needed to help get her through this. Knowing we were opposites or that things couldn't ever work out between us had no effect on the need.

It was instinct, plain and simple. And I didn't have the first inclination to fight it or even try to understand it better.

"So, you came here," I said.

She nodded. "Detective Watters knew Charlie and thought my getting out of town would be a shake-up of sorts. That the stalker would make some sort of mistake or do something that would give us a clue as to who it is."

We were still touching, so I didn't move. I wanted the connection between us. "Some of the guys at Resting Warrior are looking into it too. Jude is pretty impressive when it comes to computer stuff."

She let out a sigh. "The cops didn't find anything useful when they tried to dig into the stalker's online footprint."

"Yeah, well, Jude isn't restricted by stuff like Miranda rights and chains of evidence. If there's something to be found, he'll find it."

"Okay," she whispered. "I just want this to be over."

"I know it has wreaked havoc in every part of your life. If it's okay, the Resting Warrior guys and I are going to take turns keeping an eye on you and around here. I'll make sure you meet everyone so you recognize them."

She pulled away, and I had to tamp down my disappointment. "You guys don't have to do all of this."

"That detective sent you to Garnet Bend for a reason. Part of it was because he knows Charlie, but it was also because of Resting Warrior, I'm sure. We take care of our own."

"But I'm not one of your own."

I winked at her—actually *winked* at her; I couldn't remember the last time I'd done that to anyone. If the guys could see me now, they'd harass me to no end.

"Consider yourself temporarily adopted, City."

"City." She smiled softly, like she liked the impromptu nickname. And damned if that didn't make all sorts of different parts of me sit up and take notice. "Okay, thank you."

"I'll get your car fixed." I tapped the hood lightly. "Nothing that was tampered with will be a problem."

She reached out and squeezed my hand. I felt the same electricity I had that first day we'd touched. "Thank you for that too."

"You're probably going to get sick of having people around you so much, but after what the stalker tried with your car, we don't want to leave anything to chance. We're not going to let anything happen to you."

I knew I meant every word of it.

Chapter Eight

Jensen

Kenzie spent the rest of the day meeting half the town of Garnet Bend here in my garage. I lost count of how many times she told her story as each of the Resting Warrior guys came by.

She needed to know all of them so she wouldn't get spooked if there was a lookout in front of her apartment. Charlie helped supervise the process, and by midafternoon, we had a schedule for looking after her.

The guys' wives and girlfriends came by too, introducing themselves to Kenzie and just letting her know she wasn't alone. And God knew all of them had lived through things that allowed them to speak credibly about facing danger.

They understood what it was to live with crippling fear and wanted to make sure Kenzie knew they were available to talk to if she needed it.

I wasn't sure there was anywhere else on the planet where a group of women would have no problem with their men helping safeguard another beautiful woman.

The Resting Warrior women were completely secure in the love of their men.

"Ready for me to take you home?" I asked as I walked into the office after closing up the bays.

Kenzie was sitting in a chair, looking a little ragged. "I know I shouldn't feel this exhausted since I didn't do anything all day."

"I don't know about that. Retelling your story over and over takes a lot out of you."

She narrowed her eyes at me. "You sound like you know that from firsthand experience."

I shrugged. "A little from when I was a kid. My parents were addicts, so I constantly had to explain what had happened to me to different social workers once they lost custody of me."

Her brown eyes widened. "I'm so sorry."

"It was a long time ago." And definitely wasn't something I wanted to talk about right now. "We didn't get much lunch. Want to get some food with me before you go back to your apartment?"

"Um."

Shit. I was pushing too far.

"Sure, but I didn't bring my wallet."

That, I could handle. "How about it's my treat for having your car and leaving you stranded for so long."

She held up her hand. "You don't have to do that. I understand why you have it."

I nodded. "I know you do, but I'd still like to treat you. Call it a welcome to town, if you'd rather."

"I feel like I've gotten a very warm welcome here today, but I'll take you up on it. I'm starving."

Draper's Tavern, the local bar and grill, would be perfect for this occasion. It was a favorite in town and usually stayed busy, especially this time of the year when it was getting colder and people wanted a place to socialize inside.

There'd be music and conversations and games going on in the background, so we wouldn't have to sit and eat in silence, and I wouldn't have to struggle to find something to talk about.

It was part of why I didn't date very much. Conversation wasn't my thing.

I walked her out to my truck and drove the short way across town. I found a parking spot right near the front door, and I guided her inside. It wasn't too crowded, and Clive, the owner, saw me right away.

"Jensen! I didn't see a to-go order come in for you." He smiled at us as we walked in.

"No to-go for me today. I'm eating in with my friend."

Clive's eyes widened. "Okay, then. Right this way."

Clive seated us at a table, then Patti, his girlfriend, came up behind him at the bar and waved in our direction. She also owned one of the hair salons in town, but she helped Clive out when she wasn't busy with customers of her own.

"Hey, Jensen. And a date!" She beamed at Kenzie.

Damn it, Patti. The woman widened her eyes, gave a sheepish grin at my scowl, and retreated to the kitchen.

"Sorry about that," I said to Kenzie.

"No problem. I take it you don't usually eat here?" She tilted her head, waiting for my answer.

I studied the menu I pretty much already knew by heart. "I don't like to eat in restaurants. I prefer to take food home so I don't have to make conversation."

She looked like she was trying to hold back a smile. "I have noticed you're not much of a conversationalist."

"The only time I tend to eat with other people is during family night at the ranch. We all get together and catch up, rib one another, eat good food."

I looked up to find her studying me. "That actually sounds amazing."

"There are parts of small-town life that are pretty amazing, City. And the food here's great, even if I normally do takeout."

"Thank you for making an exception for me." She bit into her bottom lip while she looked at the menu, and I had to swallow back a groan at the sight. What I wouldn't give to be the one doing the biting...and licking and sucking.

Fuck. Now, I had another problem.

"I'm happy to be here. Thank you for making me seem more personable to the rest of the town, rather than the grumpy mechanic."

She smiled. "We'll make a people person out of you yet."

I doubted that, but I decided not to argue.

We turned back to our menus until Patti came over a few minutes later to take our orders—thankfully without mentioning my normal lack of dates.

Kenzie wasn't shy when it came to food, which I absolutely loved. She ordered a burger with everything on it, a side of fries, coleslaw, and a chocolate milkshake.

I was glad that she had a hearty appetite. Maybe she'd meant it, that she let those comments slide and not bother her when trolls made rude remarks about her looks and her weight.

Kenzie had the kind of curves a man like me wanted to hold on to and—

I slapped my menu down, wishing I could turn off my not-quite-clean thoughts just as quickly. "I'll have the same."

Patti wrote down our orders. "Coming right up. Glad to have you hanging out here for a change, Jensen."

I nodded then turned back to Kenzie, to find her watching me with one eyebrow raised. "Really, you don't eat in here very often?"

"Nah. By the time I'm done working for the day, I've generally had my fill of people."

"Don't you work mostly with cars or wood?"

I shrugged one shoulder. "Yeah, but the one or two people I talk to for a total of five minutes really does this introvert in."

She laughed, and damned if it wasn't the most beautiful sound I'd ever heard.

"Have you lived here your whole life?"

"I was actually raised in Iowa."

"How'd you end up in Montana?"

I didn't like to talk about myself, but after the number of times she'd had to tell her own hard story today, I could force myself to tell mine once. "Lucas and I met when we were kids. I didn't have the best of childhoods, so I was in the foster care system for a while."

Her brown eyes clouded over. "I'm sorry to hear that."

"Addict parents. They lost custody of me when I was ten, which was honestly a relief, seeing how they'd done a shitty job providing for me up to that point anyway." That was putting it mildly, but no need to spoil our appetites before the food even got here. "I bounced around a few foster homes, then finally was placed with a permanent family when I was fifteen. The Everetts —Lucas—lived next door. He invited me to play basketball the day I moved in, and we were thick as thieves from that point on."

Patti came back with our milkshakes. I was glad for a little bit of a reprieve as we both enjoyed those first icy sips.

"It's okay if you don't want to talk about it. I totally get that."

I shrugged. "Lucas has been a wonderful friend to me. He joined the Navy and became a SEAL. I was just a grunt in the Army for a few years, no active combat or anything. Then I went into security for a while—but it was just a job, not something I saw as a longtime career. I came out to visit a few years ago and really respected what Lucas and the guys had built here."

"The respect you guys have for one another is evident in everything. Even in how you harass and joke with one another."

I grinned. "Yeah, that's bro love-talk—sparring with one another and calling one another dickwads."

She laughed, and once again, the pure sound of it struck me. Damned if I didn't want to hear it as much as possible.

"The garage came up for sale about a year ago, and I bought it. Wanted to be close by here and help out whenever I can."

I never dreamed that would involve a situation like safeguarding Kenzie, but now that I thought about it, that was exactly the sort of thing I'd wanted to be around for.

"You love it here." She took another sip of her milkshake, and I had to force myself not to stare at her lips sucking on the straw. "Despite doing takeout all the time, you love it here."

"I do. I don't think I'll ever want to live anywhere else."

She looked around again. "I was pretty resentful of having to come to Garnet Bend a few days ago when I first arrived, but it's definitely growing on me. How could it not, when you guys are going way above and beyond to help me out? That's more than law enforcement did for me back in my hometown."

"I'm glad we can help."

A few minutes later, Patti and Clive both walked our plates out to us. They chatted a minute with Kenzie, who didn't mind a bit. Unlike me, she was definitely a people person. Finally, they left, and we dug into our food.

"Do you miss Denver?" I asked after a bite of my hamburger.

"Mostly, I just miss being busy. It's hard when you lose your work, your friends, and all your activities at one time. Especially for someone like me who doesn't do great at sitting around doing nothing."

"How is your business surviving without you?"

She let out a sigh. "I have a team, so they're able to handle things, especially face-to-face interactions. The stalker has seemed to target just me, not my actual business, so that works in my favor, at least."

I made a mental note to let Jude know about that for when he started digging into the stalker electronically. Whatever it was, was personal solely to Kenzie.

"It's good that your overall business isn't suffering."

She smeared a fry through ketchup. "Honestly, I can do a lot of my work remotely. I just don't like to be out of the loop. And right now, I'm bored. I've taught my team too well, and now they don't need me. I even miss the social media stuff, where I posted about my seminars and answered questions. But Detective Watters said that's definitely a big no."

"You like social media? I absolutely hate it."

She laughed through another bite of food. "As a tool for promotion and communication? Absolutely."

I ate a few more bites of my own meal while pondering a possible solution that might help both of us. I was so lost in my own thoughts—and hell, so used to being in only my own company—that I didn't realize I'd been silent for too long.

"What's going on in that head of yours?"

I looked up from my food to find Kenzie almost finished with hers. I appreciated that she hadn't tried to force conversation out of me.

"I was wondering if maybe you'd like a temporary job."

She blinked rapidly at me. "A job?"

"Susanna and I have been wanting to promote my woodworking, but both of us are shit at social media and have no interest in doing it. I was wondering if while you're in Garnet Bend and can't do your own work, you'd be interested in helping me start this side of mine."

She sat up straighter in her chair, her eyes darting around like she was thinking hard. "Really?"

"I sort of think it would help us both out. Me getting my business off the ground, and you having something to do. Plus, you could do it at the garage, so that means less manpower needed to watch your apartment."

"I've already got cabin fever just from being stuck there for a couple days." She winced. "Do you think Charlie will approve of this?"

"He said someone should be with you at all times. And as long as you're not on your own social media, I don't think there's any harm. But we'll run it by him."

Her eyes lit up. "Oh, I love this idea!"

I couldn't stop my own smile as I finished the last bite of my burger. "I will pay you. You don't have to worry about that."

"How about a small percentage of sales? That way, it's nothing out of your pocket, plus more incentive for me to do my best work."

"Somehow I don't think you ever do anything less than your best work."

She flushed a little and looked up at me shyly. "I try to give my best at everything. I do think that's part of the reason my seminars are so successful."

"Because people recognize your authenticity," I finished for her. I wasn't surprised.

"I was going to say my enthusiasm. But hopefully I'm authentic too."

"You're both. And now I get your skills to help me launch my passion project."

We talked details as we finished dinner, and I paid for our meals. I got her out to my truck and drove her the short distance to her apartment.

"You don't need to come up," she started. "Stay in the warm truck. I'm sure—"

I looked over at her with one eyebrow raised. "Do you know how many times I heard you tell that story where you came home by yourself and found blood on your walls? We are not taking a chance on something like that happening."

She let out a little sigh of relief. "Okay. If you don't mind, it would be great if you came up. I try not to get in my own head, but I have to admit, opening a front door is still a little traumatic for me. I'm always afraid of what I might find. That's ridiculous, I know."

"Not ridiculous at all. Back when I lived with my bio parents, I never knew what state they'd be in when I got home from school. It was always stressful. It takes a while to move past that."

I jumped out of the truck and rushed around so I could open her door for her. I helped her down—glad she was wearing boots today instead of her high heels—and we made our way up to her apartment.

It didn't take long for me to establish that everything was clear inside. The unit wasn't big enough to have many places for someone to hide.

I turned to Kenzie. "Okay, looks like you're all good. Nothing to worry about here except for how to use social media to promote woodworking."

"I'm actually really looking forward to that."

"Me too. I'll see you in the morning, City." I gave her a smile and nearly bolted out the door. If I didn't, I was going to do something epically stupid like try to kiss her.

Opposites. We were opposites. I couldn't forget that.

And I definitely couldn't focus on the fact that opposites attracted.

Because every second I spent with her was proving that more true.

Chapter Nine

Kenzie

"Wait, you're going to work for this mechanic and not get paid?"

I smiled and rolled my eyes at my mother's practical nature as I rinsed my breakfast plate in the sink, getting ready for Jensen to pick me up in a few minutes. I'd called her this morning to give her an update and help keep her from falling to pieces about not knowing exactly where I was.

I hadn't wanted to tell her about the trouble Jensen had found in my car—that would just make her worry more. But talking about creating a landing page and social media for the garage and his woodworking had felt pretty safe. Especially since I was so doggone excited about doing it.

Although, evidently, Mom still had some concerns.

"It's not really about payment. It's more about having something to do while I'm here."

"Kenzie! That's not right. You can't start a job without knowing the rate. What if he doesn't have the money?"

"It's not a job, Mom. He's helping me out, and I'm helping him out."

"He's helping you out how, exactly?"

Damn it, now what was I going to say? Telling her about the

sabotage of my car was going to send her through the roof. Telling her that Jensen and a bunch of former Navy SEAL guys were so concerned about my safety that they were taking turns watching me around the clock was enough to freak me out. I couldn't imagine what that news would do to my parents.

"He's just..." I stretched my neck from side to side, trying to come up with something to say. "It's a small town here, Mom. I can't do any work. I was going a little stir-crazy, so when he mentioned needing some assistance setting up online stuff for his businesses, I was more than happy to help. He doesn't need to pay me. I have plenty of money."

My mother was uncharacteristically silent for so long, I thought maybe our call had gotten disconnected.

"Please tell me he's not in his fifties with a potbelly," she finally said.

"*What?*" I couldn't help but laugh. "No, Mom. He's around my age. He doesn't talk much, but he's been a big help with some of my car issues. He's not taking advantage of me, I promise."

And he very definitely did not have a potbelly. I didn't have to see him without a shirt to know that; those sexy Henleys he wore hinted at an impressive physique.

"You like him," Mom whispered. I could hear the excitement in her voice.

"It's not like that."

"So you say."

"This is not a vacation, Mom." I washed out my cup and set it in the rack to dry. "I'm not here to have a travel romance. I just want this stalker thing handled so I can go back to my life."

"But is he handsome? He is, isn't he?"

I let out a sigh. "Yeah, Mom. He's super hot, okay? Like, belongs on the cover of *Hot Small-Town Mechanics* magazine." I was joking, but honestly, it wasn't far from the truth.

"I'd subscribe to that."

I chuckled at my mother's muttering and hung the dish towel over the oven handle then walked into the tiny living room.

"Okay," Mom said. "Well, there's no reason why you can't have a little fun with your handsome mechanic while you're there. You haven't done much dating since Alan."

"Yeah, well, a black eye, bruised ribs, and a dislocated shoulder made me a little gun-shy when it comes to guys."

"I'm glad that rat bastard is still in jail. Do you know how many women don't press charges in situations like yours?"

It was one of the reasons I had, even though it had been difficult and humiliating. Alan had gotten two years in prison and wouldn't be out for another six months. I'd like it better if he were in there longer, but I'd deal with that situation later.

"I know. But I can't focus on Alan right now. We know he's not the stalker since he's in jail. So, one thing at a time."

"You're right, sweetie. Any good trails around there?"

I grinned. "You know, I didn't look."

"Hiking is practically walking, and walking is excellent exercise."

"And in Denver, I walked over my step quota every day."

"With all the air pollution." Mom let out a heartfelt sigh. "I swear, I don't know what I did wrong with you. It's like you're scared of the great outdoors."

I was always going to be more like my dad than her in that regard, much to her dismay. And even if I loved outdoor activities, right now they weren't an option. Not with the—

A horn shrieked right outside my window, catching me off guard, throwing me back to the horn that had blared right as I was run off the road a few weeks ago.

I dropped the phone, covering my ears as the noise continued. The world was spinning like it had that night in my car. I'd been sure I was going to die.

I crouched down, covering my head, willing the sound to stop, but it kept on.

The car was spinning, and I was sure I was going to slide off the side of the windy road any minute and roll down the ledge. I couldn't get control. I—

"Kenzie! Kenzie, are you there?"

I looked up from my crouched position. No, I wasn't in a car. I was in my apartment. There was no horn blaring.

I crawled over to where I'd tossed my phone in my panic.

"I've got to go, Mom." My voice was hoarse, breathless.

"Are you okay? What just happened?"

"Nothing. I dropped my phone. I'll call you tomorrow, okay? I love you."

I disconnected the call before my mom could press the issue. There was nothing she could do about whatever panic attack had just come over me, and she would just worry.

I let out a yelp when I saw the time. It was already nine o'clock. Jensen would be downstairs to pick me up.

I rubbed my hand against my eyes. Hell, it was probably him who had honked to let me know he was here, and then my brain had totally blown it out of proportion.

I hopped up and grabbed my jacket, still struggling to get my heart rate under control. Yet another thing this stalker had taken from me: my ability to distinguish fact from fiction.

I headed out the door, feeling a little safer knowing a couple of the Resting Warrior guys had put up a camera in my hallway for security, and rushed down the stairs. Still, I kept my eyes open for anyone lurking. The hall was empty, and when I opened the lobby door, I burst out into the sunshine.

Jensen had parked, getting out of his truck to approach me. Just the sight of him calmed my nerves, but I refrained from running to him after being spooked.

"You didn't have to honk. A text would've been fine." I smiled, joking.

He furrowed his brow, clearly confused. "I didn't honk."

I almost tripped in my step as I reached his passenger door. "Really?"

"What am I, fifteen years old?" He opened the door to his truck for me. "What kind of grown-ass man honks for a woman to come out to his vehicle? I will come up to your door, so from now on, you wait for me."

I stared at him. Those were the most words with the most intensity that I'd heard from Jensen. He obviously took my safety seriously.

"Okay. I just heard a honk and thought it was you." *And I let it send me into a nightmare spiral that I am still recovering from.*

He walked back around to his side of the truck and got in. "I didn't hear any honk. But either way, just wait for me or whoever's coming to pick you up, okay?"

"No problem." I tried to keep a smile on my face even though I was still sweating a little from my panic attack.

"You okay?"

"Yeah. Just..." I didn't want to get into my imaginary horn craziness with him, especially not when I was this unsteady.

I forced out my brightest smile, the one I saved for when I had a real estate client who was about to drive me insane but I couldn't make that fact known. "I'm just ready to get started on our project."

* * *

"You'll be in the main office with Susanna, so I hope that'll be okay. She loves to talk, so if it gets to be too much, just ask her for some quiet. She's used to it, and you won't offend her."

I stifled a laugh at his exasperated tone as we parked at his garage. I'd already experienced some of Susanna's bright personality when we'd gone for coffee my first full day in Garnet Bend. I was a pretty upbeat person, but she was way beyond my level.

I smiled at Susanna as we walked inside. She was on the phone already, using earbuds that connected to the landline. Jensen gave her a nod, and we continued on past her, to a smaller office area.

"She's on the phone a lot, so I thought my office might be better."

I looked around. It was neat but bare. A laptop sat on the small desk with a notepad and pen holder beside it, nothing more.

"I obviously don't use this office a lot." He shrugged, indicating for me to sit. "Like I said, I'm not great with computers and online stuff."

The small room had windows, and I liked that I could see Susanna in the bigger office if the door was closed. Windows also looked out to the garage bays, so I would see Jensen too.

He got me situated and provided the log-ins he wanted to use on social media, plus some ideas he'd jotted down.

"Will this work? Can you read my scribble?"

"Sure, this will do fine."

He grimaced at the notes he'd handed me. "I'm not trying to tell you how to do your job with this. These were just my thoughts."

I studied the words he'd written on the paper: bold fonts, earth-tone colors, manly.

The last word was underlined three times.

"You know, just add whatever design you think would work to show the services and prices, an FAQ section, et cetera. Whatever you think works."

"But make it manly." I grabbed a pen on the desk and underlined the word again, grinning. "Got it."

His own grin was sheepish. "Yeah. No pastels or twirly fonts."

I bit back my laugh. "None. Scout's honor."

This was going to be fun.

"Let me show you some of my woodworking. I have a bay here that's just for that."

"Sure, show me where the magic happens. That will be good fodder for the website and social media."

We walked out to the far end of the garage, and he opened a bay door. I had to do a double take at what I saw.

"Wow. This is not what I was expecting."

He walked over to a large workbench, which was pretty much the only thing in the bay that I could name. "More than you were expecting?"

I had to chuckle. "I knew you were doing more than carving stuff with a whittling knife, but yeah. This is impressive."

"I've grown it over the past year. I use the table saw all the time. And this is a band saw."

I grabbed my phone and started typing in the words he was saying so I could look them up when I got back to the computer. "Keep going."

He flushed a little. "Isn't this boring to you?"

"Not at all. I don't know what any of it is for, but I can research that later. But this can definitely be a part of the social media campaign." An idea was already formulating in my head. "We could concentrate on a different machine each week. Talk about what it's used for."

He looked around, a smile building on his face. "I never thought of that. You're really good at this social media stuff."

"I just try to get into the heads of your customers. Tell me more."

He walked around, pointing to different things—drum sander, spindle shaper, clamp rack, jointer, radial arm saw—and I typed as fast as I could.

We finally came to a table that held what I'd been expecting: knives. All kinds and sizes.

"I'm assuming this is where it began."

He nodded. "Yes. Although I don't want that on social media."

"Are you sure? I think people would love hearing how this all got started."

He shook his head. "No."

"If you're worried it's not interesting, don't be. People love origin stories. Even things we don't find interesting, they usually do."

"I got my start in woodworking with this knife right here." He picked up one of the smallest and most unassuming of the lot.

I definitely wanted to take a picture of that. It would be great for the "About Us" page. Surely someone here had a high-end camera I could use. The camera on this burner phone wasn't the best.

"I don't want it on social media because I was ten years old, locked in my room, and hoping I wasn't going to have to use it as a weapon against my own parents."

Chapter Ten

Kenzie

What could I even say to that?

I didn't have to say anything, because Jensen continued, looking down at the knife. "That's how I got my start in woodcarving. I spent a lot of time alone in my room, and I never knew if they were going to try to come in and take something of mine to see if they could sell or trade it for drugs."

"I'm sorry."

He shrugged and set down the knife. "I started with little pieces then got better from there. By the time I was an adult, I was carving much more elaborate stuff. But my carving knife was, first and foremost, a weapon for a little kid who didn't have much security."

I swallowed hard. "Then I can understand why you don't want any of that on social media. We can manipulate the narrative a little, if you want. Just say you started carving as a child and that this was the knife you used."

The rest of his story would probably sell a lot more pieces—people loved trauma—but I didn't have to ask Jensen to know that wasn't going to fly.

"Maybe. We'll see." He stepped away from the table. "Do you have enough to get you going? I've got to get to work."

I hated that we'd lost all the enthusiasm that had lit his face when we'd first walked in here. "Yeah, I definitely have enough to get started."

"Okay, then I'll see you later."

Without another word, he left the workshop bay. I made my way back to the office, chatting to Susanna for a couple minutes. She was surprised but delighted to hear what I'd be doing. I was glad she didn't feel like I'd be stepping on her toes.

I spent the next few hours familiarizing myself with what little online presence Jensen did have for his work and thinking about color schemes and manly fonts. I kept hoping to talk to Jensen again, although I had no idea what I would say, but he kept himself busy out in the bays.

He didn't even come in for lunch. Susanna went and grabbed us all sandwiches from the deli. She and I ate together, but she swore Jensen's absence was nothing personal. He generally only came into the office to get coffee.

By midafternoon, I decided to take a cup of the brew out to him. I didn't necessarily think he was overtly avoiding me, but I didn't want to take a chance on it growing into that.

Plus, I wanted to show him what I'd done and make sure he felt it was on track.

I didn't think I'd ever used a coffeemaker so...antiquated. Now I understood why Susanna took breaks to go to Deja Brew in town for the good stuff. At least the machine still seemed to work. The process was the same. Grounds, water, and a cup to collect the liquid. The brew smelled so strong, it could've been used to fuel a damn car. I blinked, needing to step back from the steam wafting from it.

When my pot was done, I walked back to the front office to see Susanna.

"Want coffee?" I jerked my thumb in the direction of the break room.

Susanna made a face and mocked a gag. "Ugh. Hell no. I never touch that thing if I can help it." At my alarmed look, she laughed. "It's clean. I use it for an emergency dose of caffeine on long days, but that behemoth of a coffeemaker just makes it too damn strong!"

I grinned at that. "How does Jensen like his brew? I thought I'd take him a cup."

She raised one eyebrow. "Black. Simple, like the man himself."

Jensen Chambers might be quiet, but he wasn't simple, that was for sure. The more I learned about him, the more I knew that was true.

I poured him a cup, grabbed the laptop, and headed out to the garage. When he turned to acknowledge me, wiping his hands on a rag he had tucked into the waistband of his pants, I had to bite back a groan of appreciation. Okay, maybe it wasn't a tool belt with no shirt, but the man was still damn sexy.

I cleared my throat. "I made you coffee. Susanna mentioned you also drink some in the afternoon."

He took the mug. "I drink it at all hours of the day and night. Thank you."

I took a sip of my own. "I just want to make sure we're okay. I don't expect you to hang out with me in the office, but…"

He nodded slowly at me. "Talking about my parents is tough for me. It's not a place I let myself go very often."

"I appreciate you sharing what you did with me. And I want to assure you that none of it will end up public. If you ever decide you'd like to make your history part of your company's story, we can certainly add that in. But otherwise, it's nobody's business but your own."

He nodded again. "Thanks for understanding. How has it been going for you today?"

"Got time for me to show you a few things? See how you like them?"

He walked over and made a space on a worktable for me to set down the computer. A couple moments later, we were in deep discussion of fonts and colors and manliness.

If nothing else, the bright-pink curlicue font I'd set up as a practical joke broke the tension between us.

"I think we should go with the pink," he said with a smile once I showed him the other possibilities.

I had to laugh. "We actually might be surprised at how effective that would be—it would certainly be unique. But I think sticking with more traditional creatives is probably better. I'll get back to it."

An email came in on his garage account from a potential customer as I was finishing showing him what I'd worked on.

He opened it. "This is from old Mr. Rickles in the next town over. He wants me to fix up his 1981 Cadillac El Camino, but he wants to be in on it. He's had it for decades, so it means the world to him."

It didn't surprise me at all that Jensen had a reputation as someone who'd let an old man sit in on repairs. It was definitely a story that could be used on social media, but I'd bring that up later. We'd skirted enough edges for today when it came to what was okay to post.

"El Camino? I don't think I've even heard of that vehicle."

"It's pretty unique. Half car, half truck."

He pulled up a picture, and I froze, my shoulders tightening and my hands going clammy.

I'd seen a vehicle like that before. Several weeks ago. But I'd forgotten about it until right now.

"Kenzie?" Jensen put his coffee down and gripped my elbow. "What's wrong?"

I didn't take the time to wonder just how good he was getting at reading me. I was too caught up in a memory. "I, uh, just realized where I've seen one of those before. The night I was attacked in the parking lot."

Jensen guided me to sit down on a bench. Then he dragged a chair in front of me and sat down too. "Talk to me."

He placed his hand on my knee, and I briefly closed my eyes, savoring his touch. It was intimate but not inappropriate. And even if it was inappropriate, it was helping me stay centered and not fly apart, so I didn't care.

"I was coming out of my office. The sun had already set. We have so many lights in the parking lot, I thought I would be okay." I swallowed hard. I didn't let myself think about the specifics of this too often. "I was almost to my car when someone hit me hard from behind, knocking me to the ground."

I could still remember the burning pain in my palms and knees. I looked down at my palms now, almost expecting to see blood.

"Before I could get up, the stalker poured a bunch of gasoline all over me, then took off. It hurt like hell on my cuts, and I was so busy trying to get it out of my face that I couldn't even think of going after him."

Jensen's jaw was granite as he looked at me now. "It's good that you didn't go after him. You could've been killed. Jesus, Kenzie, one match and..."

"Yeah, believe me, I thought of that." It had been the only thing I could think of as I'd made my way back inside the office and tried to wash off the gasoline as best I could. "Putting gas in my car still triggers me a little."

"But you think you saw an El Camino there that night?"

I nodded, closing my eyes to concentrate. "Yes. I don't know that the stalker was driving it, but that vehicle is unique enough that I would've noticed it if it was around the parking lot regularly."

"What color was it?"

"I—I don't know. I don't remember a color. It was dark, and I wasn't focusing on it. I just remember the weird shape now. I'm so stupid not to have focused more on what was around me."

"Hey." He reached up and cupped my cheek gently. "None of that talk, City. A sudden attack like that can cause our brains to freeze up. You survived. That's the most important thing."

I leaned into his hand. "Thank you."

"I'm going to call Charlie and Jude and fill them in on this. It's a long shot, but El Caminos are relatively rare compared to other makes and models. Maybe we'll get lucky."

I hoped so. But between this and the horn that had freaked me out so badly this morning, I wasn't feeling very lucky at all.

* * *

The rest of the afternoon passed slowly, but I kept busy plugging away at the website and socials to keep myself distracted from any more thoughts of stalkers and attacks.

When I was done, Jensen was going to have a stellar online presence. It would be easy for him or Susanna to do the upkeep once it was all established.

And heck, it might be a reason for Jensen and me to keep in touch after I left Garnet Bend. But I wasn't going to think about that now. I was already still pretty shaken by all of today's triggers.

By the end of the day, when Jensen told me he'd take me home, I was having difficulty keeping my anxiety at bay. Being at the garage all day with him and Susanna had given me a sense of security, but I didn't look forward to going back to the apartment and being alone.

Where else could I go, though? I didn't have any friends to hang out with, and I wasn't going to venture around town by myself. Not that I had a car anyway.

I didn't mention any of that to Jensen, though. He was not my babysitter, despite having comforted me earlier.

"I've got an idea," he said out of the blue, breaking the silence on the ride to my apartment.

"I'm all ears." Literally. If it meant not being alone, I was up for it.

"Would you like to come to family dinner?"

I blinked, surprised by his offer. "Your family?" Everything he'd told me about himself had suggested he didn't have any family.

"Sort of. Out at Resting Warrior. Whoever's around gets together weekly to hang out and catch up. Just spend time together as a family."

A slow smile spread across my face, and I was warmed by his thoughtfulness and consideration for my situation. I was so glad to have somewhere to go where I wouldn't be alone.

And spending more time with Jensen would be a bonus I didn't want to pass up.

"Are you sure no one would mind? I don't want to intrude as a stranger."

"They won't mind at all, but I can call and ask, if it would make you feel better about coming."

I glanced at him then took a risk by reaching for his free hand and giving it a quick squeeze. "If you're sure it won't be a problem, I'd love to come. Truthfully, I wasn't really looking forward to going home to an empty apartment. So, thank you for saving me from that."

Jensen squeezed my hand back in return. "You'd actually be saving me. I'm the lone bachelor hanging out with a roomful of happy couples. For once, I won't be flying solo."

Chapter Eleven

Kenzie

I couldn't stop my jaw from dropping when Jensen drove through the gate at Resting Warrior Ranch. It was massive and intimidating. The guys here certainly took their security seriously. I could definitely appreciate that, and I felt calmer being here already, given the added protection.

Just to appease me, Jensen had called Lucas and put the phone on speaker when he asked if they'd mind if I tagged along. Not only did Lucas agree, I could hear several women yelling in the background for me to come. I couldn't help but smile at the friendly acceptance I was receiving from relative strangers.

The ranch itself was stunning. The main lodge was huge, with a couple of barns positioned off to the side, surrounded by horse pens and walkways that branched off in several directions. A large, two-story newer structure was set back farther from the lodge in the distance.

I could hear a variety of animal noises from several directions, and I spied rooftops in the distance through the trees, which had to be homes. My Realtor eye also couldn't help but notice the landscaping and added plants and flower beds scattered around and the big garden off to the side. They had really put a lot of time and effort into making this place something beautiful, functional, and homey all at the same time.

The people who came here to help recover from PTSD must immediately find it calming. Just looking around as we walked to the door, I knew I did.

"This place is amazing. Do all your friends live here?"

"All the guys used to when they were single. Now, since they're either engaged or married and a couple have kids, most have moved off property. Daniel and Emma still live on-site with their little boy, Tyson."

Suddenly, the lodge doors were thrown open, and the two women I'd met the first day at Deja Brew stood there with huge smiles to greet me. The shorter woman with the bright clothes and multicolored hair—Lena?—pulled me into a quick hug.

A laugh sounded at my side, and I turned to see Evelyn shaking her head at her friend. "Sorry, Lena's a hugger. It's good to see you again, Kenzie."

Lena scrunched up her face. "Yeah, sorry about that. I should have asked first. But I'm so happy to see you here with Jensen. He's never brought anyone with him before, so it's extra exciting that you're here."

My eyes widened at her announcement, and I glanced over my shoulder and met Jensen's gaze. He didn't seem the least bit embarrassed at Lena's statement. The opposite, in fact.

I felt my cheeks heat, but that had nothing to do with embarrassment either. Although, I hoped no one would notice.

"Come on, you two. Get in here," a male voice called from inside. I thought it was Daniel. I had spent a lot of time talking to him yesterday.

"Yeah, it's almost time to eat. We don't want everything getting cold," Liam replied from the kitchen.

The inside of the lodge was just as impressive as the outside —warm and inviting. We were the last ones to arrive, so everyone made their way to the dining area, carrying dishes of all shapes and sizes. The amazing scents wafting through the air had my mouth watering. I wasn't much of a cook, but I loved to eat.

But even better was the gathering itself. There was really no rhyme or reason to anything. It was a happy, loving, chaotic mess of good conversation and laughter among friends who were obviously as close as family.

There were kids around too, although I couldn't necessarily tell who belonged to whom since whenever a child needed something, the nearest adult handled it. All the kids were obviously as comfortable with every adult present as they were their own parents, because not one of them balked.

The chatter and cheer never waned as they all passed dishes around. Even Jensen was talking, his face as relaxed as I'd ever seen it.

And they threw me right smack in the middle of all of it, never treating me like a victim or asking me questions about my case. I was just one of the family. For someone who'd grown up with no siblings, it was a little overwhelming, but in the best way.

Conversations grew quieter as the men started clearing off the table and taking dishes to the kitchen and returning with dessert. My eyes almost bugged out of my head at the thought of eating more.

But, of course, I did. Because I was not going to miss out on homemade apple pie when it was available to me.

After dinner, the talk became a little more subdued. Evelyn and Emma disappeared to put their little ones down in one of the bedrooms. The guys, once again, started removing dishes from the table and stayed in the kitchen for cleanup.

I sat at the table, still finishing my dessert, when Lena sat down next to me. "How are you holding up, Kenzie?"

"I'm doing all right. Stuffed, though. The food and company

were both excellent. I can't thank you all enough for letting me crash your evening." I smiled, taking a bite of pie.

"You're welcome here anytime you want to come. You don't even have to be Jensen's date—although we love that you are." Lena smiled in kind. "He's never brought a date here before."

"Yeah, the owner of the bar where we ate yesterday seemed pretty shocked to see Jensen staying, especially with company in tow."

"Oh, I know Clive and Patti were thrilled. Patti was gushing about it at her salon today. News is already getting out about the hot new couple."

I felt my face heat. "Jensen and I aren't a couple."

She grinned. "Maybe not, but don't doubt that we all saw him looking at you way more than was necessary tonight. He's pretty enamored of you."

"I don't know about that. He's just the type of person to help someone out if he has it in his power to do so."

"True, true. Jensen is definitely that way. Hell, all the Resting Warrior guys are. But it's more than just that with you for him, believe me."

I didn't know how accurate that was. But I did know that I couldn't stop thinking about my handsome mechanic.

I dropped my volume. "Even if that's true, Jensen and I are too different."

"Oh honey, there's nobody in the world more different from me than my Jude."

I raised one eyebrow at her. "You mean because he doesn't have purple and teal streaks in his hair?"

Lena let out a laugh. "That, and almost every other possible way. But trust me, the differences can be what makes a relationship so great. Opposites attract, and all that."

I looked up to find Jensen watching me again with those sexy, dark eyes. I squirmed a little in my chair and shot him a smile. Opposites attract, indeed.

"Even so, I won't be here long. My job and life are back in Denver."

She reached over and squeezed my hand. "Not every relationship has to be a forever one. Maybe you can just enjoy some... *engine grease* while you're here."

Maybe I could. The more I got to know about Jensen, the more I wanted to know. "Yeah. Engine grease is definitely growing on me."

"And the stalker stuff? How are you holding up?"

I pushed my empty plate away from me. "It's been a lot, especially today. But the guys have been very kind to offer to help."

"Safety is a big thing for them all. They don't like to see any woman in danger."

Jude called Lena over, and she hopped up to respond to him. He kissed her and whispered something that made her laugh then waggle her eyebrows at him.

Love damn well permeated this place. Not just love between the different couples, although that was evident. Love between the friends, both male and female.

Love between them because they were a family. Not bound by blood—but bound by *choice*.

Suddenly, I realized how long it had been since I'd been truly able to enjoy the company of my own friends or family because of the stalker. It felt like forever.

As much as I enjoyed spending time with Jensen and his family, I was homesick for my own. I had an overwhelming need to hear my mom's voice.

I had just spoken with her earlier in the day, but I missed her. If I could just hear her voice for a minute, I'd feel better.

I stood and walked toward the hallway. I squeezed Lena's arm as I passed by her. "Excuse me. I'm going to make a quick call."

She nodded, and I made my way into the quiet hallway, hitting speed dial for my mom.

I frowned when the call went straight to voice mail. Mom always kept her phone on her in case of an emergency at the park where she worked as a ranger. It wasn't uncommon for hikers to get lost, and she was one of the first people contacted when that happened, no matter what time of day or night it was. She even kept a charger on her uniform belt so she never ran out of battery when she was at work.

Maybe she was just busy. Her not answering didn't have to mean anything nefarious. Trying to quell the worry churning in my gut, I called my dad.

His phone was off too.

Weird... I kept my breath steady, refusing to freak out. Maybe they were together and just couldn't get to their phones at the moment.

I tried my mom one more time. This time, the call was picked up. Thank God.

"Mom?"

No response.

"Mom, are you there?"

But it wasn't my mom's voice. It was a man's voice, sounding tinny and strange.

"If you care about anybody but yourself, you need to stay away from Colorado."

Chapter Twelve

Jensen

I carried more plates to the kitchen, where Jude and Daniel were doing the dishes and Lucas was standing to the side, organizing some of the leftovers.

"Thanks for letting Kenzie come tonight," I said to the room at large. "She needed it."

"How's she doing?" Lucas asked, glancing up at me as I stacked more plates near the soapy water.

I glanced out to where Lena had been sitting and chatting with Kenzie last. All night long, I'd been getting used to her by my side. But I felt like she could appreciate a little space, so I decided to help clean up. I didn't want to hover, but I was surprised that she wasn't there at my glance.

Where'd she go?

"All right, I guess." I didn't want to tell anyone that I suspected some of her cheerfulness was a front. All of this was really starting to weigh on her, which was totally understandable.

I turned to Jude. "Any update on the El Camino front?" He'd been the first person I'd called after Charlie.

"Nothing so far, but I'll keep digging. That style vehicle is unique, but there're more of them out there than you'd think. Plus, not all of them are legally registered, so I'm looking through other channels too."

"Okay, thanks for doing that."

Jude nodded. "Anything to help, man. You know that. None of us want to see Kenzie suffer."

I didn't either. Watching her remember that attack in the parking lot had been painful. She had been struggling to keep it together.

Being here tonight had seemed to help—or at least take Kenzie's mind off the stalker for a little while. I hadn't been surprised that she'd fit right in.

Although I had to admit, it scared me a little with how good it had felt to have her at my side. To casually and innocently touch her when we were passing food. How she'd reached out to smack my shoulder lightly when I'd whispered a sarcastic comment during someone's story.

She was so outgoing and chatty and sweet that I felt like having her as my date made up for my tendency to be somewhat antisocial. The gang here was used to it, but I didn't have to worry if I was being too quiet with Kenzie around. She was so bright, drawing everyone to her.

I looked out toward the table again. Still not there.

I left the kitchen to find her. I needed to see her. Something in my gut wasn't sitting right.

I checked the bathroom first, but I didn't find her. As I passed each of the ladies, I asked them if they'd seen Kenzie. Normally, I'd be a little concerned about the knowing looks they were giving me—obviously, they loved that I was asking about her—but right now, I just wanted to find her.

She wouldn't have left. Hell, she had no way of leaving. But why wasn't she in with everyone else?

I stuck my head into the main hallway to see if she was

standing out there, but I didn't see anyone. I was heading back inside when I heard a muffled sob.

"Kenzie?"

She was crouched on the floor in the hallway next to the supply closet. She sat huddled with her back to the wall and her knees tucked up to her chest, chin resting on them. She was staring at her phone.

My worry spiked, and I rushed to her side, dropping down on my knees. "Hey, City. What's wrong?"

She didn't even look at me. She pressed a button on her phone then brought it to her ear. After a few seconds, she removed it and hit a button again.

Then she repeated the process.

"My-my mom…"

I didn't understand what was happening here. "You're trying to call your mom?"

She still didn't look up. "I called her. I called Dad. They're not answering. But then… But then…"

She repeated the process with her phone, obviously trying to get through to one of them.

"Okay, hang on. Let's not assume anything's wrong. Maybe they're just busy. They're watching television or something and can't hear their phones. Maybe—"

"I called my mom first, and she didn't answer. Which is weird. She always has her phone. Then I called my dad and got no answer."

"Scary, but there's probably a perfectly good—"

Now, she finally looked at me. "When I called my mom back, a man answered. He had some sort of weird electronic voice."

What the fuck?

Kenzie's breathing was coming way too rapidly as she talked. "He said, 'If you care about anybody but yourself, you need to stay away from Colorado.'"

Holy shit. I leaped up, grabbing Kenzie's hand and pulling her along with me, running back toward the main section of the lodge.

"Lucas!" I yelled as we reentered the great room.

I didn't talk much, so when I spoke, people usually listened. I put enough urgency and volume into that one-word shout that the whole house went silent, and everyone turned our way.

"What?" Lucas ran up as I pulled Kenzie into my side. "What happened?"

Daniel was right behind him.

"The stalker might have Kenzie's parents. She called her mom, and a strange man answered with a threat about staying out of Colorado."

The Navy SEALs inside my friends broke free—you could almost see the change come over them as they went into fight mode. It had been years, almost a decade, since most of them had been active duty, but that didn't matter.

The warriors inside them still lived.

Daniel had Charlie on the phone in a matter of seconds and was filling him in on what had happened. Lucas was asking the other guys who they knew in Denver who could get to Kenzie's parents' house as soon as possible.

"Zodiac Tactical has an office in Denver," Jude responded. "I'm on it. They'll have someone out there as soon as possible."

"Meanwhile, I'll try emergency services in Denver," Liam said, all traces of his normal merriment gone. "They won't like that there's not an overt threat, but I'll see if I can talk them into sending a unit by the house."

If anyone could talk them into it, it was Liam. He was definitely the most charming of the group.

Kenzie's eyes were wide as she watched everyone in movement all around her. The guys peppered her with questions—her parents' address, exactly what the guy said on the phone, her parents' phone numbers.

The men weren't the only ones helping. "I'll keep calling Kenzie's dad to try to get through," Evelyn said.

Lena nodded. "I'll do the same with her mom."

Jude put his hand over the mouthpiece of his phone. "Have a second phone ready to record in case the stalker answers again. Any details will be helpful."

I pulled Kenzie closer to me and kissed the top of her head. "It's going to be okay."

She didn't answer, but at least she wasn't shaking the way she had been before.

The phone rang in Daniel's hand, causing her to jump. He put it on speaker so we could all hear. "Charlie."

"Watters is having an officer drive to the address now."

"Okay. We've also called Zodiac Tactical and emergency services to see if we can get someone there. Better to have more than needed."

"Agreed," Charlie responded. "Whoever hears first, update the other."

"Roger that," Daniel said.

The tension was thick surrounding us as we lapsed into silence, while my mind raced with questions. Maybe someone had paid a stranger to make the threat? A machine to disguise it? The stalker himself?

Kenzie still leaned against me. She didn't want to sit down—I couldn't blame her for that—so I just stood with her and lent her my strength as best I could.

And I prayed I wouldn't need to lend it while Kenzie got horrible news.

The minutes stretched by intolerably long, but finally, Daniel's phone pinged on the table with a text. Kenzie's nails dug into my arm as we waited for Daniel to read it.

"They're okay!" The room erupted in cheers, and Kenzie all but sank into me. "The officer Watters sent got to them first and found them at home. They're fine. He's going to have your mom call on his phone."

As if on cue, Kenzie's temporary phone rang. Her hands were so shaky she almost dropped it. I gently took the phone, pressed the accept button, and held it up to her ear.

"Mom?" She grabbed the phone.

I could hear her mother's panicked voice. "Kenzie? What's going on? Christ Almighty, I was terrified when this officer showed up. He said to call you right away."

"I..." Kenzie was still gripping her phone with white knuckles. "Where is your phone, Mom? Dad's phone? I tried to call you both."

She glanced at me, almost sheepish, and I nodded. I didn't blame her for leaving it at that. She probably didn't want her parents to worry about that threat she'd heard, especially until we had more details.

"Can you believe it? I lost my phone earlier today. I was just doing paperwork, finishing up stuff at the park, and it was gone. Or maybe it fell out of my pocket when I stopped to get gas on the way home."

But it hadn't been either of those things. We both knew that. Someone had taken it.

"I called Dad too," Kenzie said. "His also went straight to voice mail."

"Christian, where's your phone, honey?" Kenzie held the phone away from her ear as her mother yelled to her father.

It took a few moments before Kenzie's mother spoke again. "Oh, sorry, sweetie. He put it back in his office then it ran out of battery. He's charging it now."

"Okay, well, you need to get yourself another phone to replace yours," Kenzie said.

"Well, it might still show up."

Kenzie glanced at me, obviously searching for a reason to give her mom for getting another phone immediately without giving her the truth. I shrugged. I wasn't sure what was best in this situation. Obviously, she and her parents were close, but she didn't want to tell them what had happened.

"I tell you what, just get a temporary phone like the one I'm using so we can be in touch with each other, okay? Then if you find yours, the temporary one could be for emergencies or something."

Plus, Kenzie was going to need a new one, too, since the stalker now had this number. I would make sure that happened.

"Yeah, that's a good idea. I'm sorry we worried you, sweetie. But I'm going to go so this officer doesn't have to stay here any longer."

"Okay. Call me tomorrow when you have the new number. And tell Dad to keep his phone charged."

"Will do, sweetie. And don't you worry about us. You just keep enjoying spending time with your handsome mechanic."

I smothered my grin as Kenzie's face turned beet red. I was glad no one else around us could hear what her mother had said.

But I was damn sure glad I could. And that she'd mentioned me to her mother.

"Yeah, Mom. I love you guys. Call me tomorrow." She pressed the button to disconnect before her mother could respond.

We looked up to find everyone watching.

"Everything good?" Lucas asked.

"Yes, Mom's phone has been taken—obviously—but she just thought she'd lost it. My father is a little bit of a scatterbrain and let his battery go dead." She looked over at Lena and Evelyn. "Thank you for trying."

"We're just glad they're okay, hun," Lena responded.

"I explained the situation to the Zodiac Tactical guys," Lucas said. "Sarge is going to set stuff up so they can keep an unofficial eye on your parents."

"Sarge?" Kenzie asked.

"Harrison McEwan—goes by the name Sarge," Lucas explained. "Works for Zodiac Tactical, a world-renowned private security company."

"Why would he do that for me? He doesn't know me at all."

"But he knows us. He and his now-wife, Bronwyn, hid out here for a while when some shit went down for them. He's happy to help out."

"I am very thankful. For you guys, too." Her tone was completely sincere, but her face said she still didn't understand why everyone was doing this for her.

"That's how things work in a small town, City," I whispered in her ear. "We look out for each other."

"I talked to Charlie some more," Daniel said. "They'll be investigating the theft of your mother's phone. Without it, there's not a lot that can be done. The stalker is trying to scare you."

Kenzie rubbed her forehead. "Well, it's working."

"They've got protection on them now, Kenzie," Lucas said softly. "And you've got protection here. It's going to be okay."

"Would you like to stay here tonight?" Daniel offered. "I'd hate for you to go back to an empty apartment and think about this all night."

Lena grinned. "We can make a slumber party out of it." The other ladies added their agreement.

"Thank you, but no. I'll be okay." Kenzie smiled sweetly. "I'm just glad my parents are safe."

After more reassurances from everyone, we headed out. Kenzie was quiet next to me, exhaustion damn near pouring off her. As we pulled into town, I couldn't seem to stop the words that came out of my mouth.

"Stay with me tonight."

"What?"

"I know you didn't want to stay at Resting Warrior. They

meant well with their offer, but I'm sure you didn't want to be around a group of people you don't know very well."

Shit. Not that she knew me much better.

She didn't immediately reply or react. At the next light, I darted a quick glance in her direction. I found her staring right at me with a pensive look on her face.

"I just don't want you back at your apartment feeling alone and scared. Don't want to give your stalker that satisfaction, even if they don't know it."

She still didn't respond.

"Forget it. It's fine. I'm not trying to make things awkward."

I was about to turn toward her apartment complex when she touched my arm. "Yes, please. I'd like to stay with you."

Chapter Thirteen

I pulled up in front of my apartment, hoping I hadn't left my place a mess. I hadn't been planning on any company. I wasn't overly messy by nature—not always having a room of my own as I was growing up had kept me from tending to be too cluttered.

"This is me."

"Hmm." She scanned the space and nodded.

"What?"

She shook her head, still looking around.

"No. You've got something on your mind." Was she worried it wasn't safe enough here? "This is probably not quite as secure as your building since you have a lobby and interior apartment door, but I've never once had a problem here."

"I'm not worried about safety. I was just noticing the trees and flowers along the path and the fact that these buildings have a stone facade. Both add value."

My lips twitched as I led her up to my unit. "You can't turn the real estate part of you off, huh?"

"No," she admitted with a shrug. "It's impossible."

"Everywhere you go, you see it through a Realtor lens?"

"Occupational hazard. You're probably the same way with cars."

She stood behind me as I opened the door and stepped inside, not just for safety purposes but for me to give it a once-over and make sure I hadn't left any underwear in the middle of the floor.

Thankfully, nothing embarrassing. My place was clean and minimalistic in design. Just the way I liked it.

She came in and looked around. I wondered what it looked like through her eyes. The Realtor's eyes. The *woman's* eyes.

I had a few photos of myself and my adoptive family and a couple of nature prints I'd gotten from Grace Young, one of the Resting Warrior guys' wives. She and Harlan lived on a ranch property a little way away from Resting Warrior. At a family dinner at their place, I'd noticed some paintings sitting around and asked about them, and I was surprised to find out how good of an artist she was.

Lena was always threatening to take some of Grace's paintings to a gallery and see if she could find her an agent. But Grace wouldn't hear of it. She did it for pleasure; she didn't want money. But I hadn't wanted to just take them for free, so she and I had worked out a trade: paintings for automotive care.

Kenzie was still looking around. She hadn't said much. I wasn't sure if that was a good or bad sign.

"You can have the bed. I'll take the couch."

"I don't mind the couch."

I shook my head. After what she'd been through today, she deserved to be able to sleep in a bed. It wouldn't be the first time I'd slept on a couch. Hell, I'd spent half my childhood sleeping on the floor.

"No, I insist. You take the bed."

The fact that she didn't argue was testament to how worn down she was. She just nodded.

"I've got some spare bathroom things here." I pointed at the basic essentials like a toothbrush and toothpaste in the bathroom. The guys had had extras from a camping trip, and somehow they had gotten stashed here.

I stopped at the linen closet and pulled out a couple of clean towels.

She clutched them to herself like a lifeline. "Thank you."

I nodded, trying hard to ignore the warmth from her soft hand on my wrist.

"Anything else you need?" Being a host was an alien concept for me. I rarely asked anyone over, definitely not a woman. My one-night stands weren't frequent, and when they did happen, I went over to their places. I didn't want people here.

Yet, with Kenzie, I hadn't even hesitated.

"I'm good, really. I just appreciate your letting me stay." She gave my wrist a brief squeeze before releasing me.

"Oh." I gave her a quick once-over, realizing she probably wouldn't want to sleep in her jeans and blouse.

I motioned for her to follow me to the dresser, where I chose the smallest T-shirt I had. The gym shorts I picked up next would drop from her waist, but the drawstrings could help secure them if she rolled up the waistband. "These may be more comfortable."

Her smile was so sweet, it was all I could do not to pull her into my arms. Standing in my bedroom with her felt risky enough. But tonight was not about any sort of attraction. It was about helping her know she wasn't alone.

"Thanks, Jensen. This means a lot to me."

"If you need anything, let me know, okay?" I grabbed a shirt and sweats for myself before leaving the room.

"I will," she said softly as I closed the door behind me. "Goodnight."

"Goodnight."

I stood there at the door for a moment, staring at the panel of wood.

All through brushing my teeth in the bathroom and changing, I shoved back thoughts of her. I refused to envision her changing. I tried my best not to think about the image of her sliding under my covers and laying her head on my pillows.

Of what she looked like wearing my clothes.

I settled onto the couch with a spare blanket and pillow and prayed for sleep. I was wide awake, though, taunted by the idea of her so close, just on the other side of the wall and in my bed. I tried to walk through projects at the garage. Parts that were on order and vehicles that would be coming in for service.

I even started running through my custom woodcarving orders. I had several jewelry boxes, a few animals, and a set of chimes to work on next week. I was excited about trying my hand at more complex pieces like a rocking chair or end tables sometime in the near future. That would be a challenge I hadn't tackled yet.

None of that made me sleepy.

Thinking about work got me wondering about that damn El Camino, and I had to force myself to stop going down that path. If I started thinking about the stalker, I'd never be relaxed enough to rest.

And while I would take all of this off Kenzie's plate in a second if I could, I had to admit it'd been nice as hell to have her with me at family dinner tonight.

Even though I enjoyed going to family dinners at my friends' homes, sometimes I avoided them. It was a lot, seeing all the love and experiencing the laughter and the closeness when I was alone.

I'd always been content with my bachelorhood. But sometimes, in my more vulnerable moments, being around my friends and their women had me longing for something more.

Not to mention, being with them reinforced that I was not a

great conversationalist and tended to be antisocial. Mumbling one-word answers was sometimes the most I could do. I was well aware that I was never going to be the life of the party. I worried that it wore on my friends.

I hated that I felt that way. Lucas was like a brother to me—and the others too, by extension. They'd proven over and over that I didn't need to change, that they accepted me the way I was. And I appreciated that more than they would ever know.

But watching Kenzie with my friends... She fit in like she'd always belonged. I envied her ease of conversation and general enjoyment of being around them. It felt good being with her there, like she was my partner—balancing out my taciturnity.

I'd never really believed in opposites-attract stuff, but I had to admit that—

The bedroom door opened, cutting into my thoughts. "Kenzie?"

Her footsteps were light and quiet as she walked into the living room. "Are you awake?"

"No," I replied wryly.

She giggled.

"How come you're up?" I asked.

"I can't sleep." She stepped closer to the couch, hugging her arms around her waist.

And there it was. Her in my clothes. I couldn't stop staring. Maybe it was just a T-shirt and shorts, but they looked way sexier on her than they ever had on me.

"Why are you up?" she asked, dragging my focus back to the conversation.

"Same. Couldn't seem to get my eyes to close or brain to turn off." I rubbed my hand over my face. "What do you do when you can't sleep?"

"Think about work—properties or clients I'm representing. Or redecorate my house in my mind. Or stage my dream home."

I laughed. "I was thinking about work stuff too."

"Or sometimes..." She trailed off, biting her lip.

I cleared my throat, wishing I could lick away the bite she was giving herself while standing there in my clothes. "Sometimes, what?"

"Or I watch old reruns of *House Hunters International* until my eyes get tired."

I laughed. "Still pretty work-related."

I was beginning to see how much of a hardship not having her work was for her. Most people might enjoy a period of forced vacation, but it was a stressor for Kenzie. No wonder she'd jumped at helping out with my social media and website stuff. It wasn't her career, but at least it kept her busy.

"Yeah, I can be a workaholic."

"Well, watching television is definitely a part of your job I can help you with." I patted the couch and scooted aside to make room for her. She came close and sat while I turned on the TV and found her show.

It wasn't one that I tended to seek out. I didn't travel a lot. I liked hiking and camping, but going to Europe and seeing big, famous cities didn't appeal to me. I was a small-town guy, and after the way I'd lived, I liked the comfort of staying put and knowing I had a place to call my own.

We sat pressed together, sharing our warmth. Kenzie curled into me, tucking the blanket over her legs. I was aware of every place our bodies touched. And while the show wasn't holding my interest much, I was even further from the idea of sleep.

"*Lots of charm.*" She scoffed. "They mean lots of updates are needed to bring it into this century."

I almost smiled at her obvious disdain.

"And *commuter's dream?*" She shook her head. "That's usually code for the house is next to the highway. Loud and noisy."

I shifted a little then held my breath as she laid her head on my shoulder. Damned if that didn't feel right.

"Which house do you think they should pick?" she asked. "I say House One would be the best compromise."

One. Ten. I didn't fucking know. I wasn't sure how many houses were even in the running. "Uh, two."

All I could concentrate on was her snuggling up to me. I pushed all thoughts of taking it any further than that out of my mind. This wasn't the time. She seemed content, relaxed. That was more than enough for me.

When house two was declared the winner, she smiled up at me. "You got it."

She licked her lips, nearly pulling a groan from me as she ran a hand up my arm.

"Thank you." I held my breath as she reached forward and softly kissed me. "For letting me stay here and relax. For watching this show with me when I know it doesn't interest you."

I didn't want her sweet lips on mine out of gratitude. Cupping the back of her head, I dipped my mouth to hers and kissed her long and hard.

But I didn't let it go past that. No moving my hands to touch those curves under my clothes. No matter how desperately I wanted to. This wasn't the time.

The kiss ended and she sighed, resting her cheek against mine. That show of trust hit me deep down, and I knew I couldn't ruin this moment. I couldn't take advantage and press for anything more than a kiss.

The next episode came on, and she resettled herself against my side. A few minutes into the show, she stopped her commentary, and I knew she'd drifted off to sleep.

House Hunters had done its work again, but I didn't want her to stay here. She needed real rest after the day she'd had.

"All right, City," I mumbled quietly, picking her up and

carrying her to my room, loving the way she snuggled into me as I walked.

I felt the loss immediately when I placed her back in bed, but I pulled the covers up over her and lightly kissed her brow, wishing her a night full of sweet dreams.

I headed back to the couch, convinced she'd star in all of mine.

Chapter Fourteen

Kenzie

I couldn't stop thinking about that kiss.

Days later, it was still on my mind.

I'd kissed Jensen as a way of saying thanks. Although, that wasn't really true. I'd *implied* it was a kiss of thanks because that had given me an excuse to act on my attraction.

But then, he'd acted on his attraction and kissed me back and...

I sighed, pushing my thighs together as a flush once again worked its way up my neck and face. Yes, I was very definitely still thinking about that kiss. I touched my lips.

I didn't know that I'd ever been kissed so thoroughly. And what had made it even better was that he hadn't pushed for anything else.

Not that I would've said no.

But still, the mixture of such obvious desire with such obvious restraint on his part had been heady. Was *still* heady.

Jensen and I had been tiptoeing around it for the past three days. It hadn't happened again, but it damn well crackled in the air around us every time we spoke at the garage.

"Are you sure?" Jensen asked, his eyes locked with mine.

Hell if I even remembered what we were talking about. We were back at Draper's Tavern for dinner since neither of us had had any plans for how we would eat tonight. "Um, what?"

He took a bite of his pasta. "Are you sure there was a pause when that guy spoke from your mom's phone?"

"Oh." Right. Stalker. The reason I was in Garnet Bend, which did not involve Jensen Chambers's lips in any way.

All had been quiet on the stalker front for a few days. My parents were safe, and I was talking to them daily on the new burner phone Jensen had gotten me. Mom's phone hadn't been found. The Zodiac Tactical friends had reported in daily. There didn't seem to be anyone suspicious watching my parents either at home or their jobs. And I had received no messages or any further threats from the stalker.

It had been both a blessing and a curse. I was very glad for the reprieve, but it also gave me extra time to think about other things like...

I glanced at Jensen's lips as he took a sip of his beer. Yeah, I was well aware of what I'd been thinking about. I shifted in my seat again, praying he wouldn't ask if I had ants in my pants.

"Yeah, I'm pretty sure."

Without Mom's actual phone, the details of what the stalker had said hadn't proved very useful.

"But it sounded weird, right? Mechanical? Like some sort of app or software was used to change the sound of his voice."

I nodded. I'd been through all this with Charlie, who'd reported it back to Detective Watters.

"Why do that?" Jensen asked when he finished his current bite of food. "Why disguise his voice?"

I set my fork down and stared at him. "You're right."

"There has to be something distinctive about his voice that would make him want to use something to distort it. An accent, maybe, or a lisp? A low or high pitch that would be more easily identifiable?"

An even worse thought occurred to me. "Or maybe he thought I would recognize him. Maybe it's someone I talk to regularly."

The thought killed the rest of my appetite.

"I'm sorry." Jensen's face looked pained. "I didn't mean to upset you."

"You didn't." This damned stalker was the one who upset me. I picked up my fork and tried to take another small bite of my chicken potpie. It was a crying shame to let something this good go to waste.

"Watters and I have already discussed the fact that most stalkers are generally tied to their victim's lives in some way. He started working from my inner circle and moving out from there. So far, nothing. Anybody who fit the possible profile had an alibi for one or all of the incidents."

"If it's okay, I'll mention our thinking to Charlie. See if anything can be built from it."

I nodded. "Please do. At this point, I think they should be investigating anything that might narrow down the pool of suspects."

Before I could say anything else, Lucas showed up at our table, interrupting.

"Sorry to barge in," he said without humor. "But Liam thinks we might have a possible identification of the person who sent that message on your social media account the first night you were in town."

"Really?" Excited hope had my pulse racing. I wanted this over so badly, so I didn't have to stress over it anymore. Even if one of my problems could be resolved, it would be a step in the right direction.

"Can you guys come out to the ranch?" he asked, glancing at

our almost-empty plates. "Jude wants to show you. I was in town, so I agreed to deliver the message. I'm headed back there now."

I nodded, looking at Jensen.

He nodded too. "Yeah, we'll be right out."

We scarfed down the rest of our food, paid the bill, and were on our way out the door in a matter of minutes.

As Jensen drove out to Resting Warrior Ranch, I started to get ahead of myself, envisioning who this creep could be. Especially now that Jensen had mentioned using the voice disguiser.

Was it someone I knew from the seminars I taught? Could it be a client who felt jilted from not getting a property they'd really had their heart set on?

The what-ifs ran rampant in my mind, and I steadied myself with a deep breath. I was getting carried away with too many emotions. I needed to slow down and keep a level head.

Jensen noticed. In his quiet way, he reached for my hand and gave it a squeeze, like a physical reassurance to pull me back to the present.

"Hopefully this is good news."

"I hope so too." I wanted nothing more than to be able to get back to my life.

I looked down at where our hands were entwined. But maybe that wasn't so true anymore. Maybe there was something I wanted just as much as I wanted to put all this behind me.

This man.

We arrived at the ranch and went straight into the office, finding Jude, Liam, and Lucas already in the room. Jude was at the computer and ready to share the information on his screen with us.

He got right down to business. "I haven't had much luck with the El Camino, but I was able to trace that direct message you got the first night back to an IP address at a hotel in Denver."

I narrowed my eyes on the location he zoomed into on the

map. It was a national chain, huge, but nothing particularly memorable about it.

"I know that hotel, to be sure. It's on the west side of town, closer to Boulder. But I've never stayed there. I haven't dealt with the property for work either."

Jude pursed his lips. "Okay. I was hoping you'd be familiar with it."

"So, the stalker was staying at that hotel when he sent the message?" Jensen asked. "That would narrow down our search considerably. Hopefully Watters can issue a warrant for credit card receipts."

Jude looked back at the screen. "Nope, not a guest. The IP address isn't conclusive, but it looks like the message came from an employee computer."

"An employee?" I asked.

"That's why I was hoping you'd stayed there before or maybe gave one of your seminars there."

"No." I would've remembered if I had. "Most of my work is on the other side of town."

"Regardless, we've got pictures of hotel employees for you to look though." He started clicking on the keyboard and brought up another set of files. "See if anyone stands out."

There were hundreds of photos. Jensen whistled. "That's a lot."

Jude nodded. "I know. And even more because I've also included vendors the hotel deals with that might have access to their computer system. We're looking mostly at the men and anyone with records, but you should still glance at all of them."

"Okay. I'll do it." If this was a lead, I'd do whatever I could to see where it took us.

For hours, I looked through picture after picture of the people who currently worked there or had any tie to the hotel. A couple of faces stood out. They were vague, but I felt like I'd run into them before somewhere with the seminars and the courses I offered. I mentioned it to Jude, who then started to gather more information on a different computer.

But I wasn't very hopeful. I wasn't even sure I'd met them before.

"Did you ever research using this hotel for one of your seminars?" Jensen asked as he placed another cup of coffee in my hand. It had been a long evening, and my eyes were starting to cross from looking at so many pictures.

Jensen had stayed by my side the whole time. Talking things through with me when I needed it. Rubbing my neck when it had gotten stiff from holding it one way for too long.

I shook my head. "Not at this specific location. Why?"

"I was just wondering if a random inquiry about costs or dates might have put you on the stalker's radar."

"No. Although I can check with my team. I wouldn't have been the one to do that early legwork. If the hotel was out of our price point or didn't have availability on the dates we needed, I would never have heard about it."

"It's worth a try. Anything is worth a try at this point."

"It just all feels so much more personal." I set the coffee down and leaned back in the chair. "And impossible."

Jensen was standing behind me and put his hand on my shoulder. I leaned my cheek onto it, needing the connection.

"I know it does. But don't give up hope, okay? We're going to figure out who this guy is and make sure you're safe again."

I started back on the photo files, trying to take encouragement from his words. But with every passing moment, that became more and more difficult.

Chapter Fifteen

Jensen

With each hour that passed and Kenzie failed to point out any one person in the "lineup" on Jude's computer, hope sank. I wanted so badly for this to be over for her, for her not to have to constantly worry. But this was looking like another dead end.

I stayed by her side as she went through the files. Not that I was of any help, but I wanted to make sure she knew she wasn't alone.

By midnight, when she'd been at it nearly six hours, I called it. She and I had both already worked a full day, and I could tell Kenzie was starting to shut down. Her lips were pressed in a firm line, and her brow was furrowed. Every time I touched her shoulders, the muscles under my fingers had gotten tighter.

"It's time to go home," I said. "We'll have to pick this back up tomorrow."

Those big brown eyes were nearly blurry with exhaustion as she blinked up at me. "I so wanted this to provide us some information."

I kissed the top of her head. "I did too. And it still might. But right now, you're too tired to be effective. You might miss something."

Jude walked in. "Jensen is right. I'll keep trying to narrow it down, but for right now, you need to rest."

Kenzie nodded, no sign of her normal cheerfulness anywhere.

We said our goodbyes, and I walked her back to my truck. It was chilly but without the bitter winds of another impending snowstorm. The air was almost calm, in stark contrast to the unrest we were all feeling about the danger facing her.

Her stomach growled in the silence of the cab, something I normally would've teased her about. But right now, it was a symbol of how she was pushing her body too hard.

"Do you have groceries at your apartment?"

She shook her head. "No. I'll get some tomorrow."

"How about you come over to my place, and I'll fix us both a bite to eat. Then you can either stay or I'll take you home."

I was no chef, but I could hold my own with a few dishes. Tonight, it would be steak fajitas—easy and quick to make, and I'd just bought all the stuff for them. It had been hours since our meal at the tavern.

And I wouldn't even care that this would be another night when nothing would happen between the two of us. I might not be able to stop myself from kissing her again like I had the other night—especially since that kiss hadn't been out of my mind since —but I wasn't going to push for anything else.

I glanced over at her to find her biting that lip again, and I immediately turned my eyes back to the road. Damned if that didn't affect me every single time she did it.

"I'm starving, but I'm afraid I'll be lousy company."

"It's okay not to be cheerful and upbeat all the time, City. I can take it."

"It's been a long day." She rubbed the back of her neck and sighed. "I'm feeling sort of hopeless."

"Food and a good night's sleep will help. It doesn't change the circumstances, but at least it'll give you a stronger foundation to face them."

"Okay. I'll definitely take you up on your offer, then. What sort of food?"

"How about steak fajitas? I don't cook many things, but I'm pretty good at that."

She hummed in appreciation. "Perfect. It has been a while since I've had a good fajita."

We drove in silence for a few minutes. "I don't want you to be alone either."

"I don't want to be a burden. You're already doing too much for me."

"You are not anywhere near a burden. Maybe I don't want to eat alone."

She gave a short laugh. "I know that's not true. But I'll still take you up on your offer."

For the rest of the drive and then the walk into my apartment, we didn't talk, just enjoyed the silence of being in each other's company. I decided not to bring up anything to do with the stalker, hoping she would take a break and just relax. If she wanted to discuss it at all, I'd listen to her and talk it through, but I truly hoped she'd take the break she desperately needed.

Kenzie stood in the kitchen with me while I worked on my signature steak fajitas. We chatted vaguely about the kinds of foods we liked, and I wasn't surprised that she had an adventurous palate. In Denver, I was sure she had more avenues of exploration with different food varieties.

Here in Garnet Bend, if Clive didn't fix it or you couldn't cook it yourself, you probably weren't going to be eating it. It had never bothered me, but I could see how that would be a deterrent for someone like Kenzie.

But my job wasn't to sell her on a permanent life in a small town. My job was...

Hell if I knew what my job actually was in this situation. Be her friend? Help keep her safe? Provide support?

I was happy to do all of the above. But sitting in my kitchen playfully arguing about the merits and detriments of ordering sushi in a land-locked state like Colorado made me wish I didn't have to be those things. That she could be here with me under different circumstances that centered around our attraction.

Afterward, we washed the dishes together. I knew I should offer to drive her home. It was late, and we were both tired. But I just couldn't seem to force the words out.

"Would you like to sit out on the balcony for a few minutes?" I tipped my head toward the sliding glass doors that led outside. "It's a mild night, and the stars are pretty spectacular here."

"Sure." She smiled. "I don't think I could sleep right now anyway."

Living on the second floor granted me a nice, private wooden balcony. It was spacious, too. Plenty of room, even with two chairs and an outdoor love seat. I wasn't sure why I had so much furniture out here. I'd never had enough guests to fill all the seats.

"Holy crap, look at the sky!"

I had to smile as she craned her neck up to take it all in.

"We may not have sushi here in Garnet Bend, but we have other stuff that makes up for it."

"You sure as hell do. I can't see anything like this in Denver."

"Yeah, it's like that near any big city. Too much light pollution."

I sat down on the love seat and couldn't hold back my pleasure when she sat down next to me rather than in one of the other chairs. Once again, she curled against my side, but this time, we were watching the Montana sky rather than the television.

I'd take that any day. But hell, I'd sit and watch a brick wall if it meant I could have Kenzie pressed up against me.

We watched the sky for a long time. I pointed out as many

constellations and planets as I could, and we even researched a couple on my phone.

Eventually, our talking died down, and we just sat there in silence, our heads resting against the love seat's back. She let out a weary sigh. It had been a long, hard day for her.

I wrapped my arm around her. "Let's get you home so you can get some sleep."

"I don't want to go home."

"Okay, no problem. Just let me get my stuff ready for the couch so you can bunk in my room."

She tilted her head back against my arm so she was looking up at me. "I don't want that either."

She reached out, grabbing the front of my shirt and pulling me to her, kissing me.

"I don't want sleep, Jensen. I want you," she whispered against my lips.

I didn't want to take advantage of her, but I wasn't a saint. If she wanted this too, then I definitely didn't have the restraint to fight both of our desires.

The last time we'd kissed, I'd wanted to make sure she understood I had no intention of taking things further. This kiss was the opposite.

I tugged her close and pushed my tongue into her mouth to taste her sweetness. I cupped her face so I could keep her exactly where I wanted her, savoring her lips. I worked my way across her jaw to her neck.

I couldn't get enough. I found myself pulling her into my lap. Her sexy mewl as I pressed up against her drove me higher. If I wasn't careful, this was going to be over before it began.

"Can we take this inside?" she asked before pressing her lips back to mine in another drugging kiss. She slid her hand between our bodies, wrapping around me through my clothes.

I groaned, pushing my erection into her hand. She moaned into my mouth, convincing me I'd never get enough of her kisses.

"Yes." My voice was guttural, even to my own ears. "As long as we take it straight to the bed."

"Yes, please." I could feel her smile against my lips.

I slid my hand down to her ass and squeezed as I urged her to walk inside ahead of me.

"After you."

And I meant that in every wicked way there was.

Chapter Sixteen

Kenzie

I loved kissing Jensen. I loved that the very act of his lips on mine blocked out all the doubts and worries that clouded my mind.

I loved how I felt with his arms around me—safe, secure, like I could let my guard down and trust him with my care.

And while both of those things were wonderful, they were nothing compared to the heady rush I felt as I walked in from the patio. I knew he was watching me—could practically feel the heavy-lidded smolder.

He wanted me just as much as I wanted him. I was going to combust if he didn't help me get some relief.

He closed and locked the door behind us. As he turned back to me and slid his arms around me, I thought it was a hug, but when he dipped his body a bit and flexed his biceps, I realized he was picking me up.

I couldn't help the squeak that left my lips. He grinned at me, smug and sexy, knowing exactly what he was doing. Safe in his arms, I relaxed in his embrace just as he shifted me, encouraging me to wrap my legs around his waist.

The move plastered me to his solid wall of a chest and gave me a sweet hit of friction, bringing me right up against the hardness I'd gripped in my hand.

A soft groan escaped me. *Yes.* I wanted this contact. *Craved* it.

Once I locked my feet together, cinched around him, I tried my best to grind against him. I was desperate to relieve the ache that was rising to a crescendo within me.

Then suddenly, he stopped and my back hit a wall. Jensen dug his hand into my hair to hold me still and devoured my mouth. He cupped my ass harder, each dig of his fingers into my flesh ramping up my desire. At this rate, I'd combust before we made it to the bed.

I tried to grind against him harder, and his deep growl echoed through the quiet space as he assaulted my mouth in the most delicious way.

Jensen wouldn't be hurried, no matter how much more force and effort I put into rubbing against him.

It was torture, yet not.

My wicked fantasy of finally getting this man naked was a sensual experience that I did want to savor. Yet I was too desperate for relief to want to take it slow.

I wanted him inside me. *Now.*

He finally peeled us back from the wall and walked me—way too slowly, his lips still plundering mine—the rest of the way into his room. As soon as he reached his bed and set me down on the edge of his mattress, I decided to take matters into my own hands.

I stood quickly, surprising him, and pushed him back, starting to remove my jeans.

"No." He grabbed my hands, stilling my progress.

"Jensen. I want—"

"I said after you, City. I meant it." He kissed me tenderly, making my toes curl. "Let me take care of you."

My heart expanded, swelling with too many emotions I

couldn't catalogue all at once. He wanted to what now? Take care of me?

"I didn't realize I'd become your burden to take care of," I muttered as he released my hands and undid the button of my pants, pushing them gently down my legs and taking my panties with them.

"Burden?" he scoffed, reaching up to unbutton my shirt. His lips trailed kisses along my neck, and I rolled my head to the side to accommodate him.

"You think this is a burden?" He pushed his erection into me. I gasped, stunned at the exquisite pressure at my center.

"Make no mistake, City. I want you." Finished with my shirt, he moved his fingers to my bra and unclasped it. "I need you."

I shivered as his fingertips traced up the swells of my breasts. My nipples hardened as he passed them. *Oh, please. More.* I ached everywhere, but that teasing touch of his hands on my skin sent a bolt of need straight to my core.

He lifted his hands to my shoulders, shedding the last of my clothes and exposing all of me to his view.

When he picked me up and laid me gently on the bed, a fresh rush of desire claimed me. As I leaned up, resting on my elbows, he followed me down, spreading my thighs to make room for himself between my legs.

"But I want to take care of you first. I've been dreaming about touching you, tasting you, since you first showed up at the garage." His words sent a shiver through me just as much as his hand running down my waist, across my hip, and teasing me between my legs. I could feel the calluses along his fingertips as he touched my most sensitive flesh. I wasn't sure I'd ever felt anything so sexy.

I swallowed hard and closed my eyes, relishing the exquisite feeling of him touching me. I'd never been with a man who wanted to see to my needs before his own. Who wanted to focus on my pleasure before taking his.

"Does that sound good to you?"

I blinked at him as his fingers slowly glided in and out of me. Bracing himself on one arm, he hovered over me and pressed soft kisses to first one breast then the other.

"Does it sound good?" I could barely get the words out, I was squirming against him so hard. "It sure as hell *feels* good."

His smile was slow, sexy. "It feels good to me too." Then he closed his mouth over my nipple, licking and sucking at the same time he added another finger to my wet heat.

I dropped my head back and moaned, relishing the torment, pushing my hips at his hand, needing more.

"Like this?" He used his thumb to apply pressure right where I needed it, and pleasure arced through me in an almost savage wave.

I fell back on the bed, losing the strength to hold myself up anymore. He followed me down, determined to keep up the sweet torture of my breasts with his mouth as he drove me crazy between my legs with his fingers. I gripped his hair and locked his head to my chest.

"Yes. Please. So good." I could barely think, let alone speak. Never had I met a man who would check with me like this. I'd never encountered a lover who needed to see how I wanted it, how I liked it.

"I want to give you what you crave, City," he growled as he moved back to my other nipple, sucking harder and using his teeth.

"Yes." I hardly recognized my own voice. "Please, Jensen. Please."

He dipped down, rubbing himself along my thigh, and I knew he was just as turned on as I was, yet he was still fully clothed.

The thought of Jensen holding himself back for the purpose of prioritizing my pleasure made me burn hotter. He meant it. He wasn't just talking it up and making false promises about taking care of me. He was sacrificing his own release.

"I want you to come apart for me." He increased the tempo and pressure of his thumb, and I couldn't hold back the orgasm that crashed over me, ripping his name from my lips.

He didn't stop his fingers or thumb, prolonging the drag against my flesh. He sucked harder, his mouth tugging on my nipple, and made a deep, gravelly sound—one I'd daydreamed about more than once.

I scraped my nails over his scalp, sighing at the fading waves of release. He didn't retreat until I'd relaxed from his onslaught on my body.

Even as I lay there as a human puddle, I knew I wanted to make this just as good for Jensen.

He slid off his clothes and headed toward the bathroom. A second later, he came back with a condom. I watched as he slid it on and crawled back onto the bed.

"I want you inside me." My voice was low, husky, well loved.

"There's nothing I want more." He lifted my leg and aligned himself to slide into me.

I groaned with every delicious inch of him stretching me. He dragged his body against mine, spreading his kisses and stroking his tongue up my neck and over to my ear. Heat streaked through me, and I melted into him when he nipped then suckled at the tiny sting. I hugged him close as he pushed in to the hilt. Locking my legs around his waist, I focused on breathing and the wonderful friction as his body slid against mine.

"Still feel good?"

My God. He was going to slay me with his thoughtfulness.

I nodded, and he pulled out, only to drive back in slowly. Over and over, he teased my sensitive flesh.

I clung to him as the pace increased, digging my nails into his back, urging him faster. I could feel the pressure building inside me again. He growled, kissing the underside of my jaw as his thrusting increased. Before I could catch my breath, he sent me soaring into ecstasy one more time.

Jensen jerked as his own orgasm took him, and he buried his face in my neck. I rode out the fluttering sensations of pleasure, and when I came down from it all, I felt relaxed and sluggish with the inescapable tug of sleep.

All I had the ability to do was nestle into his arms. Wrapped in his embrace and curled against his chest, I was seconds away from drifting into what I was sure would be the best sleep I'd had since all my trouble started.

Chapter Seventeen

Kenzie

The next morning, my doubts crept back in. Despite how amazing our night had been and how thoroughly Jensen had seen to my needs, I felt shy and unsure how to handle the morning after.

As I blinked my eyes open and sat up in bed, I registered the delicious soreness in my body, all those muscles I hadn't used in so long. I yawned, rubbing away the grittiness of a deep sleep from my eyes as Jensen strode in.

He carried a tray of food in one hand and was balancing two mugs of coffee in his other.

"I can't say I've ever had breakfast in bed," I admitted shyly, clueless as to how to proceed with him. But the fact that he'd gone to all this trouble touched something in me.

"Glad to be your first." He winked at me and offered an easy smile. Definitely different from before. "Now, I know I wowed you with those fajitas last night, but don't hold your breath expecting anything too fancy here."

I giggled and peered at the offering. Orange juice, check. Coffee, check. He'd even brought the creamer I liked.

Scrambled eggs on the plate, I recognized. But the other blob-looking thing?

I glanced up at him, eyebrow raised.

"Believe it or not, those are blueberry pancakes." He shrugged after setting the tray over my lap, then climbed into bed with me. "I'm not that artsy."

I cleared my throat, cutting a bite. "Are they...done?"

He laughed, taking the other cup of coffee that was half drunk already. "Yeah. I taste-tested one. They're ugly but edible."

I dug in, relishing the novelty of it all. The hot man in bed with me. The delicious breakfast. Divine coffee. The chance to sleep in and not have to rush anywhere or worry—

"Oh my God." I looked over at the clock on the bedside table, almost choking on my sip of coffee and bite of pancake. "I'm late. You're late. We're late, Jensen!"

He furrowed his brow, watching me lazily.

"For work," I added, which I knew was silly. He was the boss. That implied he would be the one to determine tardiness, but still. Susanna told me that he liked to make his own hours, but he seldom came in after ten. It was close to that now.

I set down my coffee cup and moved the tray aside. "We need to go."

Before I could fully get up to collect my clothes, he slid his strong arm around my waist, trapping me in place.

"Jensen—"

He pulled me back, perching me on one knee. His tug on my midsection had me falling back on the warm, cozy bed I'd just tried to leave.

"Jensen, we—"

He lowered slowly, kissing me until I was out of breath and we were both grinding against each other. By the time he let me go, I could hardly remember what I'd been trying to do in the first place.

"I asked Susanna to open the garage for me today." He dipped down to give me another sweet, coffee-tasting kiss. "We can take our time." Another kiss, longer than the others. "I've never had a woman stay here before, so I wanted plenty of time to figure out the best way to do the morning after."

I smiled. I'd really been the first woman to stay over here at his place? I believed him—not only because I didn't think he would lie to me, but because he had no reason to.

Who would actually believe that a man who looked like Jensen wouldn't have brought women here? It was too preposterous *not* to be true.

Still… "Actually, that's not quite true." I poked him in the chest. "*I* stayed here before."

He threw back his head and laughed. God, how I loved the sound. He didn't do it nearly often enough. "That doesn't count since you slept here alone."

"Either way, we have to go into work eventually."

He gave me the most adorable pout, and we finished breakfast in an easy silence. I was glad we could tease and be comfortable with each other this morning. I wanted it again tomorrow morning.

And maybe every morning after that.

I nearly choked on the bite of my amorphous pancake at my thought. *Every* morning? That wasn't in the cards.

"I have to go home and change, though," I insisted after we got dressed and carried the breakfast dishes back into the kitchen. We'd taken a shower together, but I still needed to change. "You know Jude is going to want me to come look at the rest of those photos. I can't be wearing the same clothes as yesterday. The Resting Warrior guys are too observant. They would notice."

"Trying to hide me?"

"No. I mean…" I furrowed my brow as I tugged on my shoes. It wasn't like I was embarrassed at being with Jensen at all. The opposite, in fact. "I just mean…"

He grabbed me and pulled me to him, smiling slowly. "I'm

only kidding, City. I don't mind taking you home so you can change." We left his apartment, hand in hand. "But come straight to the garage after, okay?"

He'd returned my car to me yesterday after installing the parts that had arrived. He'd also installed a tracker and a dash camera so we'd know if anyone tried to tamper with the car again.

I gave him a goofy kiss goodbye when he dropped me off, and I headed inside to change so I could get to the garage as soon as possible. I wanted to hurry back to him as fast as I could.

"Hurry back?" I asked myself as I entered the foyer. I wasn't clingy by nature, but I was already missing Jensen.

Last night had been amazing. I couldn't keep a smile off my face even if I tried. I threw my purse down on the kitchen table and kicked off my shoes. I didn't want to waste any time not being with Jensen—no matter how unreasonable that was in the long run—so I hurried to change.

Who would've thought that I would ever be in a hurry to get back to a garage where I was working on someone else's online presence? And that I would love it so.

Yeah, this town was growing on me.

I got dressed, shaking my head at myself as I took more care than usual, choosing the jeans that particularly complimented my...*assets* and a dark blazer that I knew was both attractive and casual.

I went into the bathroom and closed the door to check what necklace I wanted to wear. My apartment had a nice pair of hooks on the back of the bathroom door, and I'd used them to drape my jewelry organizers.

With this top, all I needed was a simple chain to draw attention to my—

I stilled, my fingers reaching for a thin silver necklace. What had I just heard? I wasn't shaking and rustling my jewelry around. I strained to listen, but there was just silence. Rolling my eyes at my overzealous imagination, I turned back to select a necklace.

But a distinct jingling sound came again.

"What the..." I narrowed my eyes, realizing the sound came from behind me.

Was there a problem in a pipe somewhere? I hoped I wasn't about to have some sort of leak. That was the last thing I needed. I left the necklaces alone and turned toward the bathtub. The sound was definitely coming from there.

As I slid back the plastic curtain on the rungs, I found the source of the noise.

A snake.

A *rattlesnake*.

I froze in sheer terror.

It sat coiled in the tub, its head up and bobbing like it was testing the air. A thin tongue speared out before slithering back in. The snake did it again. The rattling increased.

Oh no.

It shook its tail as I took a step back. One foot, then another. Fear suddenly gave way, and adrenaline kicked in. Fight or flight... I was *flighting*. I spun to run to the door, holding my breath.

Oh shit.

Oh shit.

Oh—

The second I touched the doorknob, the room went dark. A faint hum stopped as the power went out, and the bathroom fan that was attached to the room's light cut off.

What the actual hell?

I blinked, desperately listening for rattling as I wrapped my fingers around the doorknob, yanking hard over my labored breathing.

Nothing.

I jiggled it, pulled again, still nothing.

I couldn't breathe, pressure building up in my throat until dizziness assailed me. My heart threw itself against my ribs.

Behind me, I heard the rattle.

That actually reassured me the slightest bit. At least the snake was still in the bathtub.

For now.

"What the hell?" My throat felt tight, and my mouth went dry. A faint thread of light glowed from the thin crack at the bottom of the door. Again, I frantically tried the knob. It didn't budge.

I was trapped in here. Alone with a rattlesnake. Cold sweat broke out along my spine. I took a deep breath and tried to hold myself together.

Think, Kenzie. Just think.

Stay calm and think!

The utter silence scared me. I blinked, straining to listen and resisting the urge to whimper. Calling out might startle the snake. No one would hear me anyway. And my phone. I patted at my pockets again, confirming that I didn't have it. I'd left it in my purse on the kitchen table.

No way to call for help. No way to get out. I licked my lips, daring to spin and face the direction of the tub. My eyes were getting used to the darkness now, and I could make out the vague shape of the tub. I didn't want to creep closer, but I had to do something to protect myself. I had no weapons, no shields. But the shower rod captured my attention.

I couldn't just stand there and hope the snake dismissed me. I eyed the shower rod, then the tub to check that the snake was still there and not on the move. I'd see it, I realized. It was a darker color than the off-white of the tub.

Eyes wide and not blinking and my heart pounding, I held my breath and crept closer to grip the rod. It was a heavy one, made of a metal that seemed sturdier than aluminum. It'd be a decent stick to beat at the snake for defense.

As I stretched to unhook the brackets from it, I realized that I'd underestimated its bulk. I stumbled, off-balance from the weight of the long length. It swung down, taking the plastic curtain with it.

The rod landed with a thud on the rim of the tub. Falling and floating after it, the curtain drifted down over the tub space.

The sound of the snake's rattle filled the room. It was no longer quiet, angered by the noise and entrapment.

I didn't know what to do.

Picking up my curling iron I'd forgotten was out on the counter, I stepped back slowly, hoisting myself up onto the counter, keeping my back to the wall. As long as I could hear the rattle, it was okay.

It was the silence that would be deadly.

Chapter Eighteen

Jensen

"Now that's quite the big smile ya got there. And I don't think it has anything to do with that miserable coffee you're staring at."

I looked over at Susanna from the second mug I'd just poured. Normally, she avoided me in the mornings since I was more of a grouch in the early hours and generally liked to be left alone. But I'd been sort of hovering around the office.

Because I couldn't wait for Kenzie to get there. Because she'd only been gone less than half an hour, and I still couldn't wait to see her.

Because damned if last night hadn't blown my mind.

"Good night?" Susanna guessed with a knowing expression.

I shrugged, unable to wipe off my smile. "Don't you have work to do?"

"Your good night have anything to do with the fact that Kenzie's not here when she's been here early every other morning?"

"I wouldn't have any idea what you're talking about." I knew my words wouldn't deter Susanna, but neither was I going to overtly kiss-and-tell. Kenzie's privacy was important to her and me.

But hell if I could wait for her to get here. Just to see a flush come over her lovely cheeks when I stared at her, both of us remembering what we'd done last night.

What I hoped to do again tonight.

I turned and went back out to the bay before Susanna could notice the physical effect that thinking about Kenzie was having on me. If I wasn't careful, I was going to have a permanent zipper imprint on my cock.

I was actually whistling as I started work on the first vehicle of the day. If Susanna heard me, I would never hear the end of it.

I got caught up in what I was doing, and it wasn't until I was wanting to go refill my coffee mug again that I realized how much time had passed.

Why wasn't Kenzie here yet?

I pulled out my phone, checking that I hadn't missed a call or text.

Nothing. My screen was blank.

I called, figuring better safe than sorry. Maybe she wanted to take a nap? Or just needed some time? It was under-standable.

The call went straight to voice mail. I debated what to do and, more than that, what to think.

She'd seemed fine when I'd dropped her off—*more* than fine. She'd seemed just as ridiculously smiley as me.

But maybe she'd been hiding how she was truly feeling. Maybe she needed space after last night.

Maybe she was regretting it all and was already trying to back out of my life.

I put away my tools, planning to call again in ten minutes. If I still didn't get an answer, I'd need to do something.

I didn't want to be too pushy. Our relationship was delicate, to say the least. I had baggage and she had a stalker, plus everything between us was so new.

"You're staring at that car like you might want to beat it to death with a wrench."

I turned and found Lucas and Liam standing in the doorway.

"Yeah." I put down the wrench. I had no idea when I'd even picked it up. "One of those days."

"Kenzie here?" Lucas asked.

"I'm expecting her any minute. Actually thought she'd already be here. I dropped her off at her apartment nearly an hour ago, and she was going to change and come straight here."

Too late, I realized what I'd just admitted. Both men stared at me with eyebrows raised but fortunately didn't say anything.

"We need to talk to her," Lucas finally said.

"About what?"

Liam walked farther into the bay and ran his fingers along the car I'd been working on. "That El Camino was a dead end."

I rubbed my eyes. "Fuck."

"Yeah," Liam continued. "Owned by an older couple who live just outside of Denver. Their son works at the same office as Kenzie and borrows it from time to time."

"Any chance he's the stalker?"

"No, solid alibis for the dates and times of almost all of the bad stuff that has happened to Kenzie."

"Damn it. I just want a lead. A direction. Any fucking clue."

Lucas crossed his arms over his chest and stepped toward me. I knew that look. Whatever he was about to say, I wasn't going to like.

"We might have one. But we need to talk to her about her ex-boyfriend."

"One in particular?" I stiffened slightly, something like jealousy surging through my veins. Her comment this morning about never being treated to breakfast in bed had made me wonder about her history. She either didn't have a lot or all the men she'd been with lacked manners.

"His name's Alan Ard," Lucas said. "He was arrested and is doing time for assault and battery."

My blood turned to ice. *Assault and fucking battery?* "He attacked Kenzie?"

"Evidently. He's been in prison for thirteen months. He'll be getting out soon." Lucas shoved his hands into his pockets.

"If he's still in, it couldn't have been him stalking her." Not that I didn't want ten minutes alone with that bastard, regardless. The thought of someone attacking Kenzie...

"No, but he might somehow be attached to what's going on. Ard has been in contact with someone at that hotel Jude found. Multiple phone calls, but they were to a different extension every time, so we haven't been able to track who he's talking to."

Liam crossed his arms, looking even more serious. "We're looking into it further, but we really need to talk to Kenzie about this."

I nodded. Enough waiting. Regardless of how she might be feeling about last night, I knew she needed to be hearing this.

"I'll call her." I did, not liking the instant sinking sensation in my stomach when she didn't answer once again.

"Voice mail?" Liam guessed.

"Yeah. Again."

Lucas frowned and lowered his arms. "What do you mean, again?"

I shrugged. "I tried calling her a few minutes ago, and she didn't answer then either. There's a chance she might not want to speak to me."

"You piss her off or something?" Liam guessed.

"No." I rubbed the back of my neck. "She...spent the night with me last night. It was good. Fine. Really great." Fuck, I didn't want to have this talk with them. My intimacy with Kenzie was our business and no one else's. "But maybe she's... I don't know. The morning after kind of thing."

"Can you use the location tracker on her phone?" Lucas asked.

I took out my phone that she'd linked to her burner. "Shows her at her place." I pulled up the other app that linked to the new tracker on her car. "Car is still there too."

We all three shared a look then moved toward the door together. Morning-after blues or not, we were going to check on her.

A few minutes later, we were in front of her apartment door. I knocked, but there was no answer. Lucas pulled out the extra key she'd given Charlie for security purposes.

I opened the door, and all three of us headed inside. All was still, but dark.

"No power?" Lucas guessed. "That's weird. Lights were on in the lobby."

It didn't look like there had been any struggle, but Kenzie's phone and purse were sitting right on the kitchen table. She wouldn't have left without them.

Lucas checked the bedroom and proclaimed it clear. Liam tried the bathroom door.

"It's locked." He knocked. "Kenzie?"

I frowned, fiddling with the doorknob. It looked like it had been tampered with, scraped and kind of at an odd angle.

Someone had messed with the door. "Get that open, now!"

Liam shouldered the door open with me right behind him.

"Kenz—" I shut up, flashing my phone's light on her curled up and sitting on the counter, hugging her knees to her chest.

As soon as she heard my voice, she turned her terrified face toward me and leaped straight into my arms. I caught her trembling body and held her tight. "Are you okay? What—"

"Get out. Get out and close the door. There's a snake!"

"What the—"

I heard the rattle the same time the guys did. We all cursed and jumped backward out of the bathroom, shutting the door behind us.

I walked Kenzie over to the couch and sat her down. Here in the light, I could see how pale she was, eyes glassy. She wouldn't let go of my arm, her nails digging into my skin.

"How long were you in there with that thing?"

"I don't know. The whole time." Her voice was barely audible.

I could hear Liam and Lucas talking about what to do, but I ignored them. They could handle this. There was no way I was leaving Kenzie, even if I could get her nails out of my arm. I shouldn't have let her come in here on her own this morning. I'd wanted to give her space, but I should've cleared the apartment first, damn it.

Lucas had pulled his weapon and was rechecking the apartment much more carefully.

"We're clear, except for..." He tilted his head toward the bathroom.

I did the same toward Kenzie. "Water?"

I wasn't about to let her go. She remained in my arms, stock-still but trembling. Her muscles were locked tight, but she shook involuntarily. Hugging her wasn't enough, but it was all I could do.

Lucas brought a glass of water to us. He tried to hand it to her, but she was shaking so hard it sloshed over the rim. I took it and held it to her lips. "Take a small sip."

She obeyed like a baby bird, so I gave her some more.

Liam was on the phone with Charlie, and Lucas left the apartment to go talk to maintenance. A few minutes later, the power came back on, and Lucas returned.

Slowly, oh-so slowly, Kenzie's muscles became less tense, and the shaking stopped. But she was still staring blankly out in front of her, not having said a word.

"Think you could help us get this thing trapped, so we can get into the bathroom?" Lucas asked me quietly.

I nodded and slid Kenzie gently away from me. She curled into a ball on the couch. I let her go and helped her resettle in the position she wanted.

I returned to the bathroom.

"She was smart, putting it under the shower curtain," Liam said. "That helped keep it contained in the bathtub."

I looked at the curtain rod lying haphazardly over the tub. "I'm not sure that she put the shower curtain over it as much as tore the whole thing down trying to get away from it."

We could all see the shape of the snake under the curtain. Every once in a while, its rattle would give an eerie warning.

No wonder Kenzie was so damn shaken. That thing was scary as fuck. Being locked in here with it in the dark?

The guys had gotten an empty five-gallon bucket from maintenance.

"I say we put this over it and weigh it down. Get someone else out here to take care of it." Liam's face was grim.

I didn't want to mess with that thing either. "Fine with me."

The rattling got louder, and Lucas had his gun out again—not that he was going to fire it into the bathtub unless it was a last resort. We all took steps closer.

"On three," Liam said. "Don't let that fucker get me. One, two, three."

I'd never seen Liam move so fast. The bucket went down over the snake, and I put weight on it to make sure it wouldn't get out.

The thing was pissed now. Rattling up a storm.

Lucas holstered his weapon and set a heavy makeup kit on top of the bucket so I could move. "Okay, it's not going anywhere."

The three of us looked at one another from inside the cramped space. Kenzie was lucky she hadn't been bitten.

Hadn't been killed.

Someone had left that snake in the tub. They'd deliberately cut the power and rigged her lock so she couldn't get out.

The stalker had found Kenzie.

Chapter Nineteen

Jensen

Thirty minutes later, Kenzie's apartment was filled with people.

Charlie was there with a couple of his deputies, looking for prints both in the apartment and where the breaker switch had been thrown to cut the power. Lucas and Liam had managed to get the snake fully out of the tub, and Liam had released it far outside of town.

Kenzie was still curled up on her couch, staring out at nothing. She'd hardly said a word.

"I know she's struggling, but we still need to talk to her about her ex," Lucas said quietly to me in the kitchen. "And about what happened in the bathroom."

I shook my head. "Not here. Not like this."

Lucas nodded. "Grant and Harlan have offered to come in here and set up surveillance cameras, reinforce the locks. Help so she feels safe."

I honestly wasn't sure that was going to be enough. "Let me talk to her."

I sat next to her on the couch, but she barely seemed to notice. I took her hand, holding it gently between my own.

"Hey, City. Can you look at me?"

It took a long moment, but finally, she moved her glance in my direction.

"I know this is all so hard, but we want to move forward so you can feel safer. A couple of the Resting Warrior guys—Grant and Harlan—have offered to come by and install cameras and locks."

For the first time, I got an actual response. But definitely not one I wanted.

"I can't." Her breath began sawing in and out of her chest as she shook her head emphatically. "No. I can't stay here. I don't want to stay here. I want to go home."

Her pitch was getting higher with each word, and her whole body began to shake. I picked her up and draped her over my lap. I didn't give a shit who else was here or who saw. Kenzie needed me, and that was the only thing that mattered.

She twisted her fingers into my shirt. "Please don't make me stay here. I want to go home."

Aw fuck, sweetheart. Home would be just as dangerous.

"Hey." I stroked her hair. "You can't go home. Not yet. But you don't have to stay here. I will find you somewhere to stay. How about Resting Warrior?"

She shook her head. "No. I can't be around other people and especially if the stalker keeps coming after me. There are kids that live there. Babies. I can't put them in danger."

"How about staying with me?"

"Your apartment?"

"No. Somewhere safer."

She'd already been to my place, so that might not be safe. It was obvious, based on this incident, that someone had been keeping track of her. They had known she wasn't here to lay this trap.

But I had a cabin I knew the stalker had no idea about. Hell, I joked about not bringing anyone to my apartment, but I never brought anyone to the cabin. It was a place I was refurbishing, taking my time and doing all the woodworking myself.

I wasn't done with it by a long shot, but it was usable. It was a location no one would think of, and it was remote. No one could follow us there without being seen.

"Where?"

"Remember the cabin I told you about when I drove you to the garage? I can take you there. It's not much, but it's good for op sec purposes."

"Op sec?"

"Sorry. Operational security." I rubbed her hand where it rested against my chest. "Sound okay to you?"

"Yes."

I shifted her back slightly so I could see her better. Her eyes were still unfocused and she was deathly pale, but at least she was responding. I just wanted to get her out of this place as quickly as possible. To give her a safer space to recover and rest and, hopefully, feel safe.

It took longer than planned getting out of her apartment. Lucas called Evelyn, and she and Lena came over to sit with Kenzie. Kenzie didn't necessarily talk with them, but I could tell she was glad to have the support. Meanwhile, I packed up what little stuff she had while Charlie and his men finished their duties.

Lucas and Liam followed us out to the cabin in their vehicle as lookouts and added protection, and Kenzie rode silently with me. One of the Resting Warrior guys was going to drive Kenzie's car to my garage, where it could be parked inside and kept safe.

We reached the cabin around midafternoon, and pulling up out front, I suddenly worried I'd made a mistake. This was a safe, neutral place for her to relax, but it also wasn't complete.

The guys stayed outside with Kenzie as I walked through to make sure it was clear. I grimaced as I tried to look at it the way she would. The whole place was pretty bare. I'd spent the majority of my time so far working on the larger parts of the renovation, rather than many details.

It was livable, but barely, and it wasn't completely furnished. It could be called minimalist at best, but it wasn't charming or inviting in any way. Currently, the furniture consisted of a few mismatched pieces just for their functionality that I'd planned to replace later. No floor coverings lay on the bare hardwood floors. I had no electronics; the space for the TV was just a huge empty space on the wall.

The state of the cabin had never bothered me. I had lived in far worse settings. Even when it was done and appropriately furnished, it was never going to be fancy. I hadn't experienced a lifetime of nice things, and I was used to making do with what I had.

But I'd never expected to be bringing someone like Kenzie Hurst here.

What would she say about this place if she saw it on an episode of *House Hunters?*

Minimalist is code for haven't put any real furniture in it yet. I could almost hear her voice in my head.

But there was nothing to be done about it now. I walked back out to them. "Okay, we're clear."

I grabbed Kenzie's bag and carried it inside, the three of them behind me. The guys took a look around, neither of them seeming too fazed at its state. Neither did Kenzie, although probably more because she was still in shock. She went and sat on the couch, curling her legs under her.

Lucas's phone rang, and from the corner of my eye, I saw her jump. She was definitely still wound way too tight.

I approached the old couch and eased down beside her, keeping my tone gentle. "You okay there, City?"

She swallowed hard, her neck straining, but leaned slightly toward me. I saw her position as a silent ask for support, so I took a risk in draping my arm around her shoulders. Then I held my breath. Waiting.

She was still stiff, but she slanted into me more.

Okay. That was good progress for now.

Lucas stepped back into the room. "That was Charlie. He spoke to Detective Watters. Let him know what happened and that the stalker had somehow found his way to Garnet Bend. We all agreed that Kenzie staying here is the best plan."

I squeezed her shoulder, and she nodded, at least listening to the conversation, which was more than she'd been capable of at her apartment.

Lucas grabbed one of the kitchen chairs and carried it into the living room, putting it down near Kenzie but not so close that it would make her uncomfortable.

"We also talked about Alan Ard, Kenzie," he said softly.

"Alan?" Kenzie jerked and exhaled a harsh breath at his name. "Why? He's not the stalker. Alan can't be the one who's behind this."

"Because he's still in jail for assault?" I asked as gently as I could.

"You know?"

I tilted my head at the guys. "Lucas told me earlier today. I'm so sorry you went through that, City. Can you tell us what happened?"

"Does it matter?"

Lucas leaned back in his chair. "It might. If you don't mind sharing as much as you're comfortable with, it could possibly help. I promise we'll explain."

She took a few deep breaths. "I met Alan at a real estate firm—the one I was at before my office now. Long story short, my career took off, while his didn't. He started taking his anger out on me. First, it was negative talk. Then it escalated. He ended up getting fired for his behavior at work, and we broke up. Then one night, he attacked me."

I wanted to punch my fist through one of my very solid wood walls, even knowing it would do much more damage to my hand than it would to the building. I saw Liam cross his arms over his chest from where he stood in the doorway, and I knew he felt the same.

"How bad was it?" I could see the rage simmering in Lucas's eyes, but his tone was even and gentle. Dealing with his wife's abuse at the hands of a psychopath had given the man practice at keeping his anger focused where it belonged—on the perpetrator, not the victim.

"Bruised ribs, black eye, dislocated shoulder. Honestly, he wasn't very smart about it. I immediately pressed charges."

I tightened my arm around her. "Good."

Liam nodded. "Jensen's right. It truly is good that you did that. You'd be surprised how many people don't."

"Alan has been in prison for over a year now. He has around another year left." She closed her eyes and took a deep breath. "That's why I haven't mentioned him to anyone. He's in prison, so he can't be my stalker. I didn't want to dredge up more bad memories if I didn't have to."

I eased my hand under her hair so I could rub the tense muscles of her neck, glad when she didn't pull away. "Nobody can blame you for that."

She looked over at me. "Why do you want to know about Alan?"

"Jude discovered he's made multiple calls to the hotel where that threat against you originated from."

Any bit of relaxation she'd gotten from my rubbing her tense muscles was instantly lost. "What?"

"Maybe he's in on this and has a partner," Liam said.

Lucas let out a sigh. "I'm afraid it gets worse. When I talked to

Charlie on the way here, Watters notified him that Alan has been approved for early parole and will be getting out next week."

Now, tension coursed through *my* whole body. "What the fuck? Can't we let them know what we suspect is going on and keep him in?"

"Watters is working on it, but as of right now, he hasn't done anything illegal. Says he's been calling multiple hotels to see about possible jobs once he gets out."

Kenzie slumped back into the couch. "I honestly wasn't paying much attention to when he'd be out since I thought it was so far in the future. He was out of my life, and that was all I cared about. I've wanted to put him in the past and move on, not dwell on him."

I rubbed my thumb over her shoulder, wishing I could erase the exhaustion from her. Her voice was dull and lifeless when she spoke. She barely looked up from her lap.

"Maybe we can talk about this more after you rest," I suggested.

She nodded weakly.

"Yeah." Lucas stood and sighed. "That's a good idea."

I led Kenzie to the bedroom, not saying anything as I helped her slip off her shoes and get into the bed. "I'll be back in just a few minutes, okay?"

She nodded, looking way too frail, and I kissed her on the forehead as she pulled the covers up to her chin.

When I stepped back out into the main living space, both men looked concerned.

"Alan couldn't have been behind that snake or any of the physical attacks on her," Liam said. "Not if he's been behind bars all this time."

Lucas nodded. "Yeah. But we can't rule out the chance that he could be arranging it from there. I don't buy the *searching for a job* story with calling the hotel. Too much of a coincidence."

"Jude and I will continue to look at the hotel employees and keep reviewing all the things online," Liam said. "We'll send pictures out to you for Kenzie to look at when she's feeling more up to it."

"Is someone going to keep an eye on Alan when he's out?"

Lucas nodded. "Watters already spoke to the prison, according to Charlie. They have the parole officer's information, and one of them will be speaking with him as soon as possible. But since Alan isn't out yet, and we're looking for a bad guy who's active, nobody wants to believe he has anything to do with it."

I knew they would all be working every angle of the case and finding out more about Kenzie's ex. But with a long look at the closed door behind which the traumatized woman rested, I wished we could just end this nightmare for her now.

Chapter Twenty

Kenzie

The second Jensen closed the bedroom door behind him, I curled into a ball. Covering my head with the blanket, I tried to cry as quietly as I could. The cabin was silent, and I didn't want them to hear me break down.

I'd seen the men glancing at one another. They wanted to talk about everything and figure things out, but my brain just couldn't keep up. They wanted to know about Alan, someone in my past who was locked up and unable to get to me. Whereas I was stuck in the present. I was locked in darkness in that bathroom, perched on that sink, desperately listening for rattles.

Trying to make myself as small as possible, wondering if I would die.

All I wanted to do was vent. Scream, even. As loud and as long as I could. Release all the built-up anger, fear, and frustration. Crying didn't help. It just made me feel weak and helpless. Like I was letting my fear take over.

The low hum of their voices in the next room reminded me that I wasn't alone. Even after Lucas and Liam left, Jensen would still be here. But I needed someone right now.

I turned to my side and freed my phone from my back pocket.

I'd been too numb to register Jensen handing it to me at my apartment before we left, but I was glad he'd given it to me.

Now, at least, I could hear a friendly voice. I called Zoe first, but she didn't answer. As soon as I hung up, my phone rang in my hand.

"Leah? I just called Zoe."

"I know. I'm over here with her," she replied chirpily. "We're so glad you called!"

"Miss you, Kenzie!" Zoe hollered in the background, clearly with her as the call was on speaker.

"I miss you guys too." I sniffled, trying so hard to keep it all in. Just hearing their voices threatened to break the tears. I missed my friends so much. It seemed like forever since I'd seen them.

"Oh, honey..." Zoe cooed, the sympathy clear in her voice.

"What's wrong?" Leah asked, more direct and mother-hen-like. "I mean, I know what's wrong, but something else happened, didn't it?"

"I—" I wasn't sure what to say.

I couldn't tell them specifics. Both Detective Watters and Charlie had asked me not to discuss the case with anyone as much as possible, for everyone's safety. And it felt doubly true since the stalker had stolen my mother's phone.

"I can't really say." It was all I could manage.

"Are you hurt?" Leah asked.

"No. I got another..." I struggled with how to word it. That snake wasn't a message. It was a live, viable, and real threat. "Another *present*. But no, fortunately, I'm not physically hurt."

"Thank God," they breathed in unison.

"Wait." Leah's voice hardened with suspicion. "Could you have been hurt?"

"I— Yeah, but I wasn't."

Zoe scoffed. "And how ironic. I just got an email from that

prison number. Updating me that Alan-the-asshole would be released soon."

I nodded, even though they couldn't see me. Both of my friends had been witnesses in the case against Alan. I hadn't needed them. My bruises and injuries had spoken clearly enough for themselves as evidence.

"I just found out about it too."

"Came much sooner than I thought it would," Leah said. "I figured he'd get in so much trouble behind bars that he would be stuck there for a lot longer."

Those had been my thoughts too.

"I hate to think of him being out at all. I mean, no one wants to run into an ex, but especially not yours."

As the girls went on about how awful Alan was and then switched to everything happening at the office, I just lay there and listened.

Talking with them calmed me. They were the sisters I'd never had. I was about to hang up and get some rest when the topic changed again.

"Okay. Okay. Let's talk about *him*," Leah said.

"Him who?" I asked.

"Don't even start with us. I stopped by your parents' to drop off some mail," Leah said. "She mentioned that you're working with a mechanic."

"A hot mechanic," Zoe added. "Something about being on the cover of a magazine?"

I let out a groan. Mom knew I'd been joking about that. "His name is Jensen, and yes, he's a mechanic."

"A hot one?"

"Yes, very hot."

Hearing my girlfriends wolf-whistling about the man who'd been so sweet and was taking care of me brought out a smile despite everything that had happened today.

"Jensen is..." I sighed, and that prompted them to giggle and laugh in reply. Girl talk wasn't something I'd planned on today, but if I needed a distraction, this was the best one I'd get. "Jensen is a surprise."

"What, you didn't think some sleepy little town would have any sexy men?" Zoe asked.

"I came here to hide and lie low, not find romance. I've put a lot of faith in the police chief, and he's enlisted the help of Jensen and his friends, who are former Navy SEALs."

"Are they hot too?"

"Well, actually..."

"Taking notes," Leah said. She exaggerated her tone as though she were writing. "Hot mechanic is friends with hot former Navy SEALs. Maybe we need to figure out where you are and move there."

I rolled my eyes. I couldn't picture either of them in Garnet Bend. They were both cosmopolitan, too used to the city life.

"Just so you know, all the hot SEALs are married or engaged. So, you can stop your wayward thoughts. Their significant others are lovely too."

That caused grumbling all around.

"But seriously," Leah said. "We're glad you've found some people to help you during this time. Especially if something else has happened. You deserve a break, Kenzie. Tell us more about Jensen."

"I like him a lot. I came here for temporary security, but now that I've met him and we're...getting closer, I'm beginning to realize, when this is all over, I'll be leaving him and coming home."

"Dayum, girl," Zoe gushed. "Sounds like he's more than just a hottie."

"He's so attentive to me. So sweet and gentle and patient." I sank back against the pillows. Thinking about Jensen was much better than thinking about being trapped in that bathroom with the snake. "He's gruff, but with me, he's so tender and lo—"

I stopped before I could say the word, but it was too late. My friends both gasped.

"Loving?" Zoe finished for me. "Were you going to say *loving?*"

I rubbed my face at that slip of the tongue. It was so hard not to hope that Jensen's feelings for me ran deeper than just scratching an itch. The way he treasured me and saw to my every need...that felt like *more*.

"He's really getting to you, huh?" Zoe asked.

I nodded, again aware they couldn't see, but it felt like something different to say it out loud. Like, once the words were out there, they couldn't be taken back.

"I think he is," I finally said. "But I just can't see how it would work. I didn't come here with any plans to start a relationship. That wasn't part of the lie low and hide plan."

"Why can't you have both?" Zoe asked. "After all that hell with Alan and then the stalker, you deserve to be treated as special."

"Yeah," Leah added. "This guy isn't going to have a crazy ex or anything in his past, right? No competition? No jilted lover he's leaving to pursue you?"

"No. Nothing like that. He's a loner, not much into relationships in general, I don't think."

"But no red flags?" Zoe checked.

"No. Nothing to show he's anything but genuine."

"Would he move back to Denver for you?"

I couldn't imagine Jensen in Denver. Not when everything he knew and loved was in Montana. "I doubt it. His life is here. His business, his friends. This place is part of him. And I have to admit, I can see the appeal."

"*You* seeing the appeal of a small town?" I could hear the shock in Leah's voice.

"Garnet Bend is different." It wasn't the town itself, but the people—all 2,518 of them—who made up the town, that made it so special. "It's gorgeous, but the way everyone is helping me has been nothing short of amazing."

"And Jensen is too."

"He is." It was true. I rubbed my hand over my face again, so tired still. "But it doesn't matter. I'm sure I'm looking too far into it all."

"No!" Leah shouted so loudly I had to pull the phone from my ear. "Don't go being all negative and doubtful."

"He and I are just so...different. He's quiet, a loner, small-town. I'm more of a people person, like to be on the go, like the city."

"But being different isn't so bad," Leah said.

Actually, Jensen and I kind of reminded me of my parents. They were polar opposites, but the love between them was fierce and strong and true.

Being similar had nothing to do with it.

Would it be possible that Jensen and I could find that same sort of happiness and connection?

I knew he made me happy, made me feel safe, made me feel cherished. Could the rest be figured out?

I hung up with the girls, and as I drifted off to sleep, it wasn't that snake on my mind, but the man who had carried me out of that bathroom in his arms.

Chapter Twenty-One

Kenzie

I woke up gasping for air, the sound of the snake's rattle blending with Alan's voice inside my head. I sat straight up, hands stretched out in front of me...

To what? Ward off a blow? Stop the snake from striking? I had no idea. I just knew that fear sealed my throat and I couldn't get in enough oxygen.

"Hey, City, you're okay. Little breaths, all right? In through your nose, out through your mouth."

Jensen. Jensen was here with me. I was safe. I launched myself into his arms.

He held me for a long time. Just like he had each time all night when I'd had a nightmare.

"Water?" he asked.

"Please." He handed me a glass, and I guzzled it. I looked around as I tried to get my bearings. I had no idea what time it was. "How long have I been out total?"

"All night and most of the morning." He glanced at his watch and muffled a yawn behind his free hand. "It's almost lunchtime."

"Have you been up this whole time?" Worry filled me. He had to be worn out.

"I napped some. Did some carving." He pointed at the small box that sat on the chair.

"You've been there all night?"

"I was on the couch, but you were crying out." His face softened into an expression of concern.

"I'm sorry." I tried to pull away from him, but he pulled me back.

"No need to be embarrassed. Anyone would've had nightmares after a day like you had yesterday."

"I hate that I kept you up most of the night."

He stroked a hand down my cheek. "I'm sorry you went through what you did. I should've never let you go into that apartment alone."

Now that some of the general shock over the snake incident was wearing off—not that I wasn't going to be terrified of snakes for the rest of my life—the reality of the situation was setting in.

"You couldn't have known."

He shook his head. "When I think about the fact that the stalker could've been there just waiting for you..."

A shudder ran through us both. That was what was even scarier. That the stalker had to have been inside my apartment to sabotage the bathroom door lock and put the snake in my bathtub.

"You can trust that won't happen again," he said. "I'm not going to let you out of my sight."

At one point, that might have made me feel smothered. But not with this man. I snuggled farther into him, drawing from his strength. "Thank you."

"Lucas and Charlie are looking into Alan's release."

I nodded. "I sure wish he could just stay in my past."

"And Liam and Jude are looking into who he could be in contact with at the hotel. Alan says he's looking for a job, but that's too much of a coincidence for me," he added.

"Him or not, I just want all of the snakes out of my life." I shuddered again.

"That's going to happen. We'll figure out a plan with the guys, lie low here, and make sure you're safe again."

I had no doubt they would. But I also knew what that meant—it would be time to leave Garnet Bend. Time to leave Jensen.

I couldn't think about that now, not while I was so close to him, breathing in that unique Jensen scent that both comforted me and turned me on.

I tilted my head up and kissed the side of his neck, the only part of him I could reach. "Thank you. For everything. Just being close to you makes me feel safer."

He turned so we were facing each other more fully and cupped my cheek. "I can't stand the thought of something happening to you. I hate that you've been through so much."

I shrugged. "What doesn't kill you makes you stronger, right? You, more than anyone, know that."

"Your strength amazes me, City. I just want you to know that."

I kissed him. Not to stop his words, but because I didn't want to go any longer without feeling his lips pressed up against mine. Maybe it was the near-death experience, or maybe it was the fact that everyone was working so hard to get me out of danger.

Because when the danger was over, so would be my time with Jensen.

He returned my kiss with every bit as much enthusiasm as I was offering, leaning his weight on me and pushing me back onto the bed. I twined my arms around his neck, biting back a little groan at the feel of him hard and muscular against me.

I was reaching to unbutton his shirt when my stomach growled so loudly it almost startled me.

He broke the kiss to throw back his head and laugh. I was never not going to love the sound of that. "I think we need to feed you before we do anything else."

He was right; I hadn't eaten anything since breakfast yesterday. "Okay."

He trailed a finger down my cheek. "You go take a shower, and I'll see if I can make better pancakes than yesterday."

The shower felt wonderful. Maybe it didn't rinse away all my fear—it was going to be a minute before the sight of a bathtub wouldn't cause my heart to start hammering—but it at least helped me feel more human again.

I got dressed in jeans and an old sweatshirt and walked back into the kitchen. My stomach decided to herald my arrival by growling obnoxiously again.

He'd made bacon and eggs and slightly more traditional-looking pancakes than yesterday. "Everything smells amazing. Thank you."

I leaned up to kiss his cheek as thanks. "Kate and Noah dropped off food while you were sleeping. All the women put together some stuff for us."

"That's sweet."

"Otherwise, we'd be eating canned beans right now."

"I think I'm hungry enough that I probably wouldn't even have complained."

He slid bacon onto my plate, along with eggs and two pancakes, then made a plate for himself. We padded over to the small table. I immediately dug into my food, but he looked around.

"I'm sorry this place is so sparse. It's still in construction phase. I'm doing the work myself."

I looked around. Yes, it was definitely bare, but it had great potential. "This cabin has great bones. And the custom woodwork you're doing will just add to the value."

He shrugged, but I saw his small smile. "I don't know that I ever plan to sell it, but thank you. Good to know I'm not going in the wrong direction."

"Definitely not."

We ate in silence for a few more minutes. With most people, the quiet would've felt uncomfortable, and I would've tried to fill it. But with Jensen, I knew this was just who he was. It made me appreciate more the words he did choose to say.

Once we were done, he picked up both our plates and carried them to the sink. "I know I said this already, but I want you to know it's the truth. I'm sorry that I didn't get to your apartment sooner yesterday. I should've gone to check on you when I first realized you hadn't come to the garage yet. But..."

I waited for him to continue, but it seemed like he didn't plan to do so. "But what?" I finally asked.

"I thought maybe you'd had second thoughts about...hooking up with me the night before."

I almost choked on the coffee I was sipping. "*Hooking up?*" A wave of heat spread over my face. "Is that...all? Is that all it was for you? A hookup?"

Had I been thinking we had a real connection while he was ready to move on?

But he shook his head. "No, it wasn't. I thought that might be what you felt."

"Not at all, Jensen." I walked over to where he was rinsing the plates in the sink, standing behind him. "Why would you think that?"

He scraped the plate with much more force than was necessary. "We're just so different. I mean, look at this place. I'm a mechanic who can't figure out my own social media, and you're a highly successful Realtor. My parents were addicts. If you step back and look at it all, I just don't measure up."

"Measure up to whom?" I scoffed. "My last boyfriend is in prison for assaulting me. I think you're way ahead of the game there."

I put my hands on his waist. He still didn't stop messing with the dishes, but at least he was doing it with normal force now.

"And you had no control over who your parents were or what they did when you were a child. But you found your place as you got older. And now, you've got your own made family. A wonderful group of friends who will bend over backward to help in any way they can. I'm case in point with that. Your friends are helping me because you asked them to."

He shut off the water.

"That's family, Jensen. *Your* family. I see it all around here. It's making me wonder how I'm ever going to leave Garnet Bend."

He dried his hands on the towel hanging by the sink and turned slowly around. "Could you see yourself...staying?"

I sighed. "Even after all this craziness is over—if and when it ever is—Denver is my home. I miss my friends, my community."

This time, he took my hand and squeezed it, perhaps understanding the dilemma I felt myself struggling with. I squeezed his fingers back. "And then there's you. I'm scared of how strong my feelings are. How *quickly* they've become this strong."

"Me too, City. Me too. Watching you sleep last night, I realized how much you've gotten under my skin. But I get it. Your life isn't here."

But you are.

I furrowed my brow, wondering how I could tell him that without moving too fast.

"But, hey. We don't have to figure everything out now." He wrapped his arms around me and pulled me into his body. I wanted nothing more than to snuggle in close, so that's exactly what I did.

"Let's get rid of all snakes, stalkers, and violent exes, and then we'll figure out the rest." He ran a hand up and down my back. "In the meantime, let me take care of you."

I leaned back and grinned at him, amazed I could smile with the overall state of my life. "You already are."

He tipped his head toward the window, indicating out back. "But we could enjoy ourselves even more."

I leaned up to peer out the window, seeing nothing from my vantage point. Sometimes, it sucked to be short. "What's out there?"

"I have a hot tub installed just out back on the deck."

I blinked, surprised. "Interesting priorities. Install a hot tub before seeing to the completion of the interior."

He chuckled. "Want to take a dip with me?"

I smiled shyly. "I, uh, didn't exactly bring a bathing suit with me."

Stepping closer, he tempted me with that sexy scent that was all man, all Jensen.

"We're all alone way out here." He stepped into my space until he hugged me with one arm around my back. Leaning toward my ear, he whispered, "You don't need a suit."

Chapter Twenty-Two

Jensen

When I mentioned skinny-dipping in the hot tub, Kenzie's breath hitched. She lowered her lids, and that shy look shot straight to my gut. I didn't miss how she leaned toward me.

I'd take care of her however she wanted me to. Her comfort was key. That didn't necessarily mean sex, though.

Clothes or no clothes in that hot tub, sex would still be her call. I wasn't going to push.

"I'll go get changed. I think I left a suit here last time that I didn't use. You can decide if you want to go au naturel or find something to wear. Towels are stacked out there too. Up to you."

I turned from her, going back to the bedroom to find my suit. Maybe she was modest. Maybe getting naked in the hot water wasn't something she wanted to consider right now. She would be fine there, but I hadn't considered the vulnerability I was asking of her.

Maybe asking her to get naked out in the open air was too much. She could be focusing on needing to run to safety, an engrained instinct, not wanting to get frisky or soak like this. I should've thought about that.

As I changed, I wondered if I'd find her sitting in the swirling, steaming water or if she would just be seated near the tub, still in her clothes, debating passing on the opportunity. I was pleasantly surprised when I stepped out there and found her in it.

Kenzie sat with her long hair piled into a messy bun high atop her head. Her face glowed with a sheen of moisture. Under the lights projecting up from the bottom of the tub, shadows lit her gorgeous face, those high cheekbones so pronounced that they gave her a sense of mystery.

My heart raced. I was relieved she'd taken me up on this and had gotten in. And that relief turned into a wicked thrill when I saw she had, in fact, gone without any sort of swimsuit. I schooled my features and attempted to get my lust under control. I ordered my cock to stand down.

She looked like an angel, relaxed and smiling.

This was about seeing to her needs. Her comfort. Nothing more, just that.

Unless she wanted something else.

"You coming in?" she asked quietly.

I nodded, stepping into the water. Stinging prickles lanced up my feet and legs, but it felt good. The hot water and the cool air on the sheltered deck felt like the perfect balance. I stepped in farther, submerging more of my body and soaking in the heated liquid.

Bubbles frothed on the surface, hiding her body from view. I tried not to look. I hadn't taken enough time to learn and memorize her body when we were together, and I wouldn't ask for it now. She had to let me know if that was what she needed. With all the control I could manage, I sank in and sat next to her, letting my head drop back on the headrest as I sighed.

"This feels so good."

Her faint laughter made me smile. "I'll say."

I rolled my shoulders, trying to work out the kinks from my

night of dozing in the chair. She watched me, not quite smiling but reflective.

"Still tense?" I regretted it as soon as I spoke. Of course she was. Spending five minutes in a hot tub wouldn't erase everything that had happened in the past twenty-four hours.

"Yeah." She lifted one hand and set it on her shoulder, rubbing there.

"Let me." I raised my arm, offering for her to come sit in front of me.

Asking her to move closer felt like torture, but she accepted my offer. Water lapped toward me as she slid over. I turned slightly, going for the corner seat in the tub, and spread my legs apart so she could fit between them.

The second she leaned back toward me, her ass nestled between my thighs, I jolted at the spark of pure need that spiraled through me.

Fuck.

Thinking about her naked had been bad enough, but now, as I spread my hands over her smooth skin, I was in hot water—literally and figuratively.

Her moans didn't help. Each time I kneaded the tight areas on her shoulders, she let out the sexiest sounds of appreciation, every one of them making me even harder.

The way she tilted her head to the side, giving me more access, provided more of a view that I couldn't resist. This show of her trust hit me straight in the heart, and I warred with trying to stay on course with the massage. I was aching for more.

I blinked, stuck on the sight of the tops of her breasts, so silky and wet. I sucked in a quick breath when she pushed back into me, almost flush to my chest.

There was no way she couldn't feel me now. But she didn't seem offended. She was...

"Jensen?" She purred my name, raising her hand out of the water.

"Yeah?" I cleared my throat since my voice came out ridiculously strained. My mouth was dry. I was painfully hard. I wasn't sure how I was controlling my breathing and my desire for this woman.

She slid her hand up my arm behind her, until her fingers were resting behind my neck.

"Kiss me, Jensen." She trailed her fingers into my hair, holding my head and twisting to press her face to mine.

I didn't need any further prompting. I covered her mouth with my own, brushing my lips over hers and opening for her tongue, as she moaned into my mouth. I slid my hand underwater to press against her stomach, trying to hold her still.

Except she had no interest in staying still. She only had an interest in driving me crazy by grinding back against me, seeking me out beneath the swirling bubbles.

Turning around fully, she ended up straddling me on the hard plastic seat. Her thighs bracketed mine. Keeping her arms looped around my neck, she kissed me until we were both breathless.

Not that that took long with the way she was pressed against me, rubbing herself up and down in sensually slow lifts. If she kept this up, I wasn't going to last.

"Jensen..." She ended on a sigh, framing my face as she caught her breath. She tracked her nails down my cheeks and over my jaw, the bite perfectly painful. She leaned back and I caught her, roaming her back with both my hands. I didn't waste one second more before nuzzling my face between those sweet, tempting breasts.

She ground against me, pushing down on my straining cock. Every time I swirled my tongue around her nipple and sucked hard, she gasped and moaned louder.

"These shorts have to go. Right damn now." She sat back up

and dipped her hand underwater to grab my cock. Her hold on me wasn't dainty or shy. With a firm grip, she stroked me up and down, pushing me closer to the edge.

"Not here," I growled and kissed my way down her throat.

"But—"

I stood, holding her in my arms. Having sex in the tub wouldn't be a bad idea, but I wasn't ready for this to be over yet. She deserved more.

"I'm not done making sure I've kneaded all the tension out of you."

I set her feet down, both of us shivering slightly from the change in temperature.

"Oh, I'm relaxed," she teased, reaching out to stroke me once more.

"Hmm. I need to make sure." I sidestepped her hand and directed her to the corner where the towels were stored. If she gripped me one more time, I'd end up losing it and embarrassing myself.

I wasn't above a little tempting, though. So, before she could reach for a towel, I dropped my shorts, letting myself spring free. I could feel myself getting even harder under her molten gaze.

She stared at me and licked her lips, as if readying herself for a taste. The sight of her lustful stare was about to set me off once again. She started to lower herself to her knees on the deck, but I leaned forward and swooped her over my shoulder, and I darted inside. She let out a squeal and laughed, and I loved the carefree sound. Wanted to hear it over and over.

I stepped back after lowering her to the bed, taking my time looking over her silky skin and sexy curves as she was laid out on my bed. All naked and open for me.

She leaned up on an elbow, watching me look my fill.

"Ahem," she said. "About that tension..."

I arched a brow as she trailed her hand down between her

breasts and angling toward her hips. When her finger stroked toward the sweetness I wanted to devour between her legs, she sighed. "I'm really tense right here."

I grinned. This woman would be the death of me. She wasn't shy in telling me exactly what she wanted in a sultry, sexy manner that kicked my desire for her up another notch. She knew what she wanted, and the fact that she wanted it with me had me wishing I could worship her for the rest of our days.

Hell, if I wasn't falling in love with this woman.

I dropped onto the bed, more than ready to deliver.

"Here?" I asked, kissing up her thighs until I was between her legs. I made sure to stroke my tongue all the way up until I found her clit. "Oh yes, definitely tension here that needs taking care of."

"Ah, yes! There." Kenzie slumped back on the bed as I ravished her.

I didn't stop. After making her come twice, I gave in to her demands to fill her. As if I wanted to do anything else.

Holding her afterward, I knew this was very definitely more than just *hooking up* for me.

Looked like opposites did attract.

And now, all I had to do was figure out a way to make it last.

Chapter Twenty-Three

Kenzie

I would've never thought I'd be thankful for having a stalker who was intent on terrorizing me, but for the next three days, I was almost exactly that. Without the stalker, I wouldn't have had this time with Jensen.

Not only the time in bed together, but also the time out of it, getting to know each other one conversation at a time.

If we weren't soaking in the hot tub while we watched the snow fall out back, we were cozy inside. When we weren't tangled up in bed, tasting, exploring, and pleasuring each other, we were cuddled elsewhere in the cabin.

I was never going to be able to look at a sparse home in a negative way again. I loved the exposed beams and sharp angles of this place, and I wasn't sure how I was ever going to leave it.

Although that ultimately had little to do with the cabin and more to do with its owner—with his own sharp angles and beams.

Jensen still didn't say very much unless I asked him questions outright, and he talked a lot in grunts and one-word answers. That was growing on me too. Somehow, he'd told me multiple stories about his childhood—heartbreaking stories—using as few words as possible.

Since I'd grown up with my parents who had doted on me and treated me like a third little adult in our trio, hearing about Jensen's years of neglect and some outright abuse had been hard. No wonder he'd learned to keep as quiet as possible. Nobody had ever wanted to listen to what child Jensen had to say.

But those sad stories just made experiencing the contrast of his life as an adult even more rewarding. Whether he could see it or not, the people in Garnet Bend, particularly from Resting Warrior, *loved* him.

Yeah, they were all big former military guys, so nobody was throwing around the l-word out loud. But it was obvious in their actions.

How Noah and his fiancée Kate were helping Susanna out in the garage while Jensen was here with me.

How Evelyn and Lena had brought us food twice in three days.

How Jude and Daniel were still consistently working on my case with Charlie and Detective Watters. Not necessarily for me, but because I was Jensen's, and they would do anything for their friend. No. Not their friend, their *brother*.

I was Jensen's.

I looked over at him now, carving a jewelry box over near the fire. He'd been carving or working on something in the cabin almost every moment we hadn't been wrapped around each other.

Watching him work, the small box held so carefully in his big hands, humming almost silently, I felt something click in my heart.

I was falling in love with this man.

Honestly, I wasn't sure how I felt about that. He was someone I'd never expected from somewhere I'd definitely never wanted. Yet, here we were, with me not being able to imagine my life without him.

"Any luck?" he asked without looking up from his carving.

I returned my focus to the laptop in front of me that Daniel and Jude had brought over yesterday. I'd gone through all the male hotel employees and vendors, but when those had all proven to be a dead end, we'd switched to the females to see if any of those images would jog any memories.

"Honestly, no. Some of these people look vaguely familiar, but I've lived in Denver a long time and work with hundreds of people a week. So, I may have met them, but I don't remember anything of significance."

"You doing okay about Alan's upcoming release?"

That had been the other reason for the guys coming over. Watters had been unsuccessful in stopping Alan's parole. He would be out sometime next week.

"Yeah. He's the least of my worries. I'll deal with the bigger psycho in my life then go back to worrying about the littler ones."

"Part of his upcoming parole agreement is staying away from you, your family, and your acquaintances."

Hopefully that would be enough to truly get him to leave me alone. "Let's hope that works."

"Good."

"Speaking of, my parents want to meet you when this is over."

That got him looking up from his woodwork project. "You told them about me?"

"Yep. My friends too. Is that okay?"

He lost some of his deer-in-headlights look. "Yes. Actually, I like that."

I liked it too. My parents would love Jensen. Mom was Mom and had never met a stranger. She'd be able to coax even someone as quiet as Jensen out of his shell. My dad would talk all things mechanical with him. Computer science wasn't the same as car repairs, but I recognized that nerdy sort of analytical intelligence in both of them.

"Wait until you eat some of my mom's cooking and then see if you still feel like you like it. My mother is many things, but great in the kitchen is not one of them."

He grinned at me. "Apple didn't fall far from that tree, did it?"

I threw a pencil at him. "Watch it, buddy." But he wasn't wrong. I wasn't much of a cook.

He looked back down at his project. "Will your parents be disappointed that you're...dating a mechanic?"

There was a lot to unpack in that question. Like the fact that we hadn't actually dated yet, except for a couple meals in town. Less dating and more that Jensen had become my personal guardian angel from the moment I'd pulled into town.

But the lack of dates would hopefully correct itself once the stalker situation was dealt with. So, I decided to focus on the other part of his question.

"Not even a little bit. My parents respect hard work, first and foremost. You've got that in spades. Plus, you're intelligent and pretty easy on the eyes."

"Hey, don't forget my sparkling wit and superb social skills."

We both laughed. I shook my head. "You're not as bad as you think you are."

"I'll look forward to meeting them." He smiled, a real one. It was slow and sexy. He walked over to me and dipped low to kiss me soundly. "I'm not glad about why you came into my life, City, but I love that you did."

I sighed, kissing him in reply.

"You sit tight, finish your homework, and enjoy the fire. I'll go start some dinner for us."

I raised an eyebrow. "Afraid to let me cook?"

He chuckled. "Maybe. But maybe I just like taking care of you."

This man. I didn't know what I was going to do with these feelings. All I knew was that I couldn't imagine my life without him. We would have to figure things out.

I prayed he'd want to as badly as I did.

I closed the computer and stared at the fire as Jensen got out the ingredients to cook. I didn't want to think about the future—either the stalker or the challenges Jensen and I would face—not tonight. The sun had gone down, and I just wanted to be present in this moment.

I didn't know how long I'd sat there when I heard some sort of crunching noise outside the window. I ignored it the first time, thinking it was the fire, but I froze when I heard it again a few seconds later.

That pop again. This time, it was longer, a prolonged push of something crunching, not a quick pop of the fire roaring in front of me.

I stood up, trying to keep calm. I couldn't see anything out the window in the darkness. I was letting my imagination run away with me.

The sound I was hearing wasn't someone walking in the snow outside. Nobody was around here.

But then I heard it again.

"Jensen." My voice wobbled in a low whisper. I licked my suddenly dry lips, but I couldn't seem to make my voice work any louder. I stumbled into the kitchen.

He immediately knew something was wrong. "What is it?"

"I think I heard someone outside." I shook my head, trying to clear some of the fear. "But I don't know. Maybe not. Maybe I'm just having a panic attack."

He didn't dismiss me out of hand, which made me feel better. "Go sit on the couch. I'll check it out."

"It may be nothing," I whispered. "I just don't trust myself anymore."

He shrugged as he reached the door. "If it's nothing, then no harm don—"

He stopped as we both heard the noise this time. I watched,

holding my breath, as he crouched near the door. He grabbed a crowbar he'd placed there.

More questions filled my mind, each one more frantic and worried than the last as he reached for the doorknob.

Who was out there?

It couldn't be one of his friends, right? They'd tell him if they were coming, wouldn't they?

Was it the stalker?

Was it someone who was just lost and needed help—

I screamed as the door was kicked in. Jensen was in the perfect position to attack, but also to be attacked. The door knocked him back as a masked man burst in.

Jensen's arm was up in a block, but it wasn't enough to deflect the man's bat coming out of nowhere and crashing into his head.

"Jensen!" I screamed again, terrified as he fell to the floor. In the haze of panic and fright clouding my senses, all I could do was stare at him lying on the floor as another masked man burst inside, heading straight toward me.

I momentarily froze, not sure what to do, not wanting to leave Jensen defenseless on the floor. That moment of hesitation cost me. When I shook myself out of my daze and turned to run, the man was there, blocking my path. He grabbed me and yanked me toward the door with him.

I immediately started twisting and pushing to get away. His hard fingers dug into my flesh, causing me to cry out. I punched at him, but he caught my hand and wouldn't let me go.

Dressed only in my tank top and pajama pants, I was at a disadvantage on many fronts. Suddenly, the man jerked me hard, pulling me flush against him. I immediately froze and looked up into a pair of soulless eyes full of anger and lust. I started to shake violently from the cold and fear as I felt the man's hot breath brush across my face.

No. This wasn't happening.

Movement by the door jarred me out of my statue-like state. My eyes immediately went to Jensen lying on the floor unconscious. The tall man who'd knocked Jensen out prodded him with his boot then kicked him in the side, waiting for a reaction. Seeming satisfied Jensen wasn't faking, he walked around the other side of the couch to box me in between them.

"Hold her still, and this will be over quick," the tall man said behind me. I couldn't help the whimper that escaped.

What would be over? What were they going to do?

I was too scared to voice the question, but as soon as the shorter man in front of me shifted his grip on my arms, his hands skimmed the sides of my breasts.

I went manic. If these men were going to rape me, I wasn't going to just stand here and do nothing.

I twisted, jerking my arms, flailing around as much as I could to get a little space between us. The shorter man was caught off guard and stepped back for balance, and I had my opening. I brought my knee up as fast as I could and jammed it in his crotch, causing him to completely release me.

"Fuck!" He doubled over.

But the other man wasn't so easy. He grabbed me, yanking my arms behind my back.

"Hold her." The man I'd just kicked approached with fire in his eyes, clutching his junk. I couldn't help the small smirk that formed on my face at the damage I'd done.

"Think that's funny? Bitch!" The fist came at me too fast for me to prepare. Hard knuckles slammed into my stomach, and I bent over, gasping, trying to find air. "Not so funny now, is it?"

The man behind me yanked me back up and bound my hands tight with some sort of zip tie. Still, I kept fighting. I couldn't let them take me.

"Hurry up and inject her with that shit." The man behind me

wouldn't let me go, no matter how much I fought. The other guy pulled out a needle and stuck it in my arm.

"What was that?" I yelled.

"Nighty-night time, bitch."

A few seconds later, I felt it. I pitched forward to the couch, nausea swirling in my stomach and my eyes getting heavy. I tried to shake my head to stop myself from fading, but that only made the darkness close in faster.

I heard more rustling of fabric, heavy footsteps, and the sound of something being dragged. I felt hands on me, a cool breeze. I was moving. I tried to force my eyes open to see what was happening, but the best I could do was a hazy view like looking through a dirty window.

The short man threw me over his shoulder and followed the tall man out the door. The last thing I saw before I was carried away was Jensen's distorted form, unmoving on the floor.

I whimpered, wanting to reach for him, but I couldn't make anything move.

With my next breath, I was sucked into a dark void of nothing as everything faded to black.

Chapter Twenty-Four

Kenzie

I woke up slowly, unable to get my bearings. I'd had another nightmare, but this time, it hadn't been about the rattlesnake. It had been about Jensen lying hurt on the floor.

My heart began thundering in my chest as the memories came flooding back. This wasn't a nightmare. Or at least, it wasn't one I could wake up from.

The jostling rhythm of tires let me know I was in a vehicle, but I kept my eyes closed. I didn't want them to know I was awake yet.

Staying as still as possible, I took inventory of my body, cataloging what hurt and where. Pain radiated from several places, but overall, I felt intact. Though I knew I would have a bunch of bumps and bruises, out of all my aches, my head and stomach hurt the most. I also felt sluggish and disoriented and a little sick to my stomach.

But that was nothing compared to what they'd done to Jensen.

The last thing I'd wanted was for my family or friends to be hurt back in Denver. But I couldn't stand the thought that anything had happened to him either.

I could still see the baseball bat swinging. Still hear that sickening thud as it hit him.

I had no idea if he was even alive.

My eyes burned with unshed tears, and I tried hard to keep them at bay. Jensen couldn't be dead. I refused to believe it. He just couldn't be, not so soon after I'd found him.

He had to be okay. As soon as I got back to him, I wouldn't waste a single second to tell him how much he mattered to me. How thankful I was for him.

But first, I had to escape. I needed to focus and figure out what was going on now. How I could get away. Where was I being taken?

I forced my eyes open and wiggled my fingers. My wrists were still bound, in front of me now. At least I wasn't blindfolded or gagged.

I opened and closed my mouth, then swallowed hard. My skin was tight. My mouth was dry. I needed to get used to moving again, and while I did, I studied the two men who'd taken me.

They'd taken off their masks, and I could make out some of their features. I didn't recognize either of them, not from real life and not from any of the photos I'd looked at from the hotel. Was one of them my stalker?

Hell, were *both* of them my stalker—two people working together this whole time?

I flexed my hands, testing the strength of the zip tie and how well I could move my fingers. Not tight enough to cut off circulation, but I couldn't get much range of motion with the plastic digging into my skin.

I silently twisted and tugged but couldn't get my hands out. Whatever I did would have to be with that handicap.

I shifted my view to the door. The handle was right there, only inches from my face.

Could I open the door and jump out?

I wasn't sure I could. The way I was positioned and with my wrists bound, I'd be clumsy and slow to move. The men in the front would realize I was awake. I envisioned them slamming on the brakes. I'd be tossed forward, unable to break my fall. Then by the time I'd twist and reach for the door, they'd be on me.

Or even if they didn't, it still wouldn't work. Leaping out of a car going this fast was only going to get me killed.

But I refused to lie here and do nothing. I would have to use the only thing that gave me an advantage. My mind.

"Which one of you is my actual stalker?" I cleared my throat, desperate for water, as my words came out hoarse.

The tall guy in the passenger seat grunted, turning just enough to see that I was awake. He glanced over at his partner, a bald man, who met his eyes but kept driving. Neither of them answered.

"It obviously has to be one of you two if you kidnapped me. Why are you doing this?"

"Look, lady," Tall Man responded. "We don't know what the fuck you're talking about. Neither of us are stalkers. We don't even have any idea who you are."

"What? Then why the hell did you kidnap me?"

Silence reigned once more.

I decided to go another route. "How did you find me?"

Tall Man shook his head. "We were given the location."

Given? Okay, this was making a little more sense. These guys had been hired by someone, undoubtedly my stalker. "By whom?"

More silence.

A thought came to me. "Either of you ever been in prison?"

"Jesus," Baldie said. "What is this, twenty questions? Shut the fuck up."

"Did you meet Alan in jail? Is he the one who hired you?"

Tall Man spun to look at me. "For fuck's sake, lady, neither of us have ever been in jail. Just be quiet."

Hadn't been in jail. But he could be lying. Alan could still be behind this.

"Did Alan put you up to this?" I demanded. My voice rose with each question.

Baldie snorted as he sped up on an incline. "We don't know an Alan."

"You're telling me you don't know Alan Ard?"

"Fucking hell, woman. We don't know anyone named Alan anything."

Baldie's frustration was evident, but I still didn't know if I believed him.

It didn't matter anyway. Whether he was telling the truth about Alan or not didn't change my plan.

"Look, I'll pay you. I'll pay you more than whoever hired you is going to give you. I'll pay you anything if you just let me go."

Tall Man turned, scowling at me. "Shut up."

So, more money didn't capture their attention. Was it a matter of delivering me to Alan dead or alive? Did they care? "Have you been hired to kill me?"

"I said, shut up," the tall one repeated louder.

I ignored them and tried again. "Why are you doing this?"

"Final warning. Shut. Up." Baldie barked the order at me and caught my eye in the rearview mirror. I could see his full face in the reflection.

That couldn't bode well for me, could it? If I could identify them, they must not be planning on allowing me a chance to talk to law enforcement.

It scared me enough that I stopped asking questions. I had to figure out another plan.

Eventually, we turned off the paved road and onto a dirt path. The car bumped and jostled, and I struggled to keep myself upright with my hands bound. No buildings stood nearby. We had to be somewhere remote.

But this was Montana. Damn near everywhere was remote.

The only thing I could see in the moonlight was the snowy landscape as we drove down the rough path. We were going slowly enough that I could jump out now. But what good would that do? I was in my pajamas with no coat, only slippers. It would take them mere seconds to catch me.

Finally, we slowed, and I saw a single vehicle waiting up ahead. Through the darkness, I saw a person stepping out of the waiting car, and I stared, not able to process what I was seeing.

I realized Tall Man and Baldie hadn't been lying about Alan, if this was who had paid them to kidnap me.

It was a woman. And it was clear they were expecting to meet her in this remote spot in the middle of nowhere.

As she strode closer, a faint memory was triggered.

I knew her. She'd been to one of my workshops a while ago. Had asked some normal questions about commercial real estate. Nothing that had made me think twice about her.

I recalled my conversations with this woman, and while I struggled to place her and why in God's name she'd hired two men to kidnap me, Baldie got out and opened the back door.

I didn't have a chance to try to bolt. The door was wide open, but I was blocked by the woman striding up to me.

She lifted her arm, and before I could open my mouth to ask what the hell she wanted with me, she activated the stun gun in her hand. I cried out and jerked as my body convulsed in spasms of pain and white-hot heat.

I felt the tiny sting of a pinprick, and everything went black once more.

Chapter Twenty-Five

Jensen

I paced to the window in the office at Resting Warrior Ranch and ignored the throbbing in my head.

But damn, it hurt like a fucking bitch.

It didn't fade as I turned back and strode to Jude's desk on the other side of the room. Back and forth. Over and over. I couldn't stop thinking about Kenzie. She had to be terrified. Was she hurt?

Worse?

I couldn't even allow myself to think about that.

I pivoted too quickly and almost lost my balance. Once my head quit spinning, I started my steps again. Back and forth. There was no goddamned way I could stand still. I needed to move and burn off energy, too full of pent-up anger.

"Jensen?" Lucas asked from behind Daniel's desk, where he was staring at the computer screen. "Are you sure you don't want to go to the hospital and at least have them check for a concussion?"

I grunted, debating if I should even answer him. My reply would remain the same. *No.*

When I'd woken up at the cabin, I'd found my head a bloody mess and Kenzie gone. My heart had almost stopped as I feared the worst, but she hadn't been dead. I'd clung to enough clarity in my mind to call Lucas.

Lucas and Harlan had been in town and raced to the cabin immediately. While Lucas was helping me, Harlan did a quick search, confirming what I already knew. Kenzie was gone.

With effort, they both got me into the truck and drove back to the ranch to rally the others while Harlan filled in Charlie on the phone. He was currently off following up on a lead from the highway patrol, but he said he'd check in with us soon.

"Jensen?" Liam repeated, his tone even, when I didn't answer Lucas.

They were handling me. Managing me. I was a liability, and everyone in here knew it.

"No. There is no way in hell I'm wasting time worrying about myself." I rolled my eyes, regretting it immediately as pain pierced my skull, and started pacing again. "We need to focus on finding Kenzie."

Because of the attack at my cabin and Kenzie's kidnapping, it was now all hands on deck. A couple of the Resting Warrior guys were out of town, but everyone else was searching and calling in every favor they could to try to find her.

They'd found nothing but me at the cabin, and I hadn't seen much except a guy in a mask and a baseball bat swinging at my head. It was lucky I'd managed to get my arm up to partially deflect the blow or I'd probably be dead now.

Harlan had searched the cabin inside and out. He'd managed to find two sets of footprints in the snow but not much else.

Tracks from another car were there, but they didn't help much either. I couldn't even confirm a timeline; I had no idea how long I'd been unconscious. We had nothing to go on, but my friends were all determined to work on this from as many angles as we could.

Liam watched the security camera footage from nearly every

shop in town that had one, hoping we'd get lucky and capture an image of the vehicle that had taken Kenzie from the cabin.

Harlan was checking back through the hotel employee list. I knew I should have looked too, but with the pounding in my head, I was afraid I'd be sick if I tried. I'd only seen my attacker for a few quick seconds, and he'd had a mask covering his face. I recalled the man was tall and thin, but without being able to see his face, I knew there was no way I could match him to anyone in the records.

We'd gotten slightly luckier with the second man, a bald, stockier guy, whose image had been captured on an old camera I'd set up near the back of my cabin to catch still images of wildlife that came by. The image was blurry, but at least it was something.

Jude had contacted every computer specialist he knew to see if we could get the image cleaned up and obtain info on the man. Since he'd been outside alone, he hadn't put on his mask yet, so we might get lucky with his ID.

Jude slammed his hand down on the desk. I winced as we all turned toward him. "Finally caught a break. Got an ID on the bald guy. It's Mark Cruz."

Lucas scoffed, shaking his head. "Now, why am I not at all surprised by that?"

I turned toward him, hating how fast I moved my head. It hadn't been just my head that had taken a hit. My neck was sore too, likely from the angle I'd fallen and passed out. I wouldn't complain, though. I couldn't, not when I feared Kenzie suffering a far worse fate.

"Who is Mark Cruz?"

"A lowlife we've had a run-in with before," Lucas summed up.

Harlan nodded. "He's got a brother who's done time for assault. He's the worse of the two, but apparently Mark's making a name for himself as a criminal too."

"He was arrested a while back during the dogfighting ring

roundup, but charges were dropped. Nothing could be pinned on him directly," Liam added.

The dogfighting ring. I'd heard about that. I doubted any of them would ever completely forget that nightmare. I hadn't been around Resting Warrior at that time, but I'd heard about it later at family dinners when they reminisced. Something like that didn't ever really go away.

But considering that was how Noah and Kate and Daniel and Emma had all found each other, both good and bad memories were involved.

Jude scrubbed a hand down his face. "But Mark's got no ties to Alan Ard. Still, I'm going to call Charlie and have him head to Mark's last known address, see if we can turn up anything. It's about an hour from here."

"I'll head out there too," Harlan volunteered. "Poke around, see if there's anything to be found."

I looked at Harlan then around at the other guys, not sure if I should insist on going or not.

Lucas walked over and squeezed my shoulder. "I think you're needed here more than there. Harlan will let us know immediately if he finds anything. The chances of Mark Cruz going back to his place are slim."

I nodded, but I didn't like it.

"I'll keep you posted, I promise," Harlan said then took off at a jog out the door.

A few minutes later, Daniel walked in from the other room, phone to his ear. The grim expression on his face warned me that he wasn't here bearing good news. He hung up, shaking his head.

"What?" I asked.

"That was the prison. I wanted to set up an early-morning visit with Alan and talk with him before he was released. See what we could observe from him if he was asked face-to-face about Kenzie."

"Prison said no?" Lucas rolled his eyes. "Did you tell them Kenzie has been kidnapped?"

Daniel shook his head again. "Worse. Alan Ard was let out yesterday."

I tensed, fisting my hands, wanting to lash out. "*What?*"

"What the fuck?" Lucas said at the same time.

"Why in the hell would they release him early?" I asked.

"Evidently, the parole board had a last-minute schedule change. They ended up shifting as many cases and hearings as possible. Alan was moved up," Daniel explained.

Our frustration was shared, and we all had to adjust our plans now. We'd planned to have someone follow Alan when he got out next week. Even though the parole officer would be in contact with him after his release, we were going to make sure someone tailed him for a while. If he was the stalker, he'd make a mistake.

Lucas looked over at me. "Could Alan have been the one who caught you with the baseball bat?"

Jude pulled up an image and spun his laptop around so I could see it. Bastard was handsome in a slicked-back-hair way.

"How tall is he?"

Jude turned the computer back to himself. "Says 5'10"."

I shook my head. "Then no. I'm 6'1", and this guy had a couple of inches on me. And he was sort of skinny. Alan is more muscular."

And the fucker had used those muscles to hurt Kenzie. I wanted to put him in the ground.

"Okay," Lucas said. "So, the second guy was probably hired along with Mark Cruz too. Honestly, I doubt either of them is the stalker, just hired thugs."

"Unfortunately, the news about Alan gets worse," Daniel said. "The prison official I spoke to said that he personally didn't agree with Alan being released. He's been in for thirteen months, and for the first six, he was a troublemaking pain in the ass. Fights, even talking about how he was going to kill the people who put him in jail."

"Fuck." I kicked the leg of a chair as I paced back again. I did not want to hear that. Alan had to have been talking about Kenzie. She was the only person who'd pressed charges against him and got him arrested.

He wanted her dead.

"But then in the past seven months, his behavior improved remarkably, enough that they shortened his sentence."

"Overcrowding," Jude quipped unhappily.

"Alan was an asshole, risking a longer stay, but then he did a one-eighty and became a model prisoner," Daniel continued.

It was interesting that Kenzie's stalker problems had started about six months ago, not long after Alan started behaving himself. But Alan couldn't have been the stalker from prison, right?

Something wasn't adding up here.

But one thing I knew for sure: I didn't trust the fact that the man had changed his tune. Alan hadn't gone from wanting to kill Kenzie to model prisoner for no reason.

He'd had a plan.

"Find out anything else about him?" Lucas asked.

"Not many visitors at first." Daniel crossed his arms over his chest. "Then about eight months ago, a Jada Moyer started visiting him. She met Alan when she was visiting her brother, who is also in jail there. But then she stopped logging in to visit her brother to visit Alan instead."

"Sounds like a romance," Liam said. "And could be the reason he cleaned up his act."

Daniel nodded. "The prison official seems to think the same."

I finally gave up on pacing and slumped into a spare chair, frustrated beyond measure. I didn't give a flying fuck about this little love affair. I failed to see how this applied to Kenzie's situation.

If anything, Alan finding a new woman to have in his life reduced the likelihood that he'd want to screw around with anything to do with Kenzie. Alan moving on should be a good thing.

My friends talked on, debating how to interpret this news about Alan's release. They were all able to do something to help find Kenzie. They all had their purposes. All I could do was sit there and nurse this killer of a headache.

Beneath the throbbing pain, though, something nagged me. The more I tuned out the others and tried to pick at the errant thought that wouldn't let go of me, the louder it became.

Jada.

It wasn't too common of a name, and I'd seen it somewhere. I pulled the spare laptop over and scrolled through the hotel employee list again. I might not be able to match a picture of a man to someone in here, but if I could find this woman...

There. I slapped my hands to the desk, pulling myself up straighter.

"What? What is it?" Jude asked.

I pointed at the image that was on my screen. "Jada is a unique name. I remember seeing it when Kenzie was looking through photos of people who work at the hotel. There's a Jada Banks."

"Jude," Daniel said. "Look up what you can find on Jada Banks."

Within a few seconds, he was rattling off info. "Moyer was her maiden name. She's divorced, but she never went back to it. Yep, brother's name is Moyer too." His fingers clicked rapidly on the keyboard. "And yep, Jensen was right. She's a PR associate at the hotel we've been looking into."

We all looked around at one another, one by one.

"Holy shit," I muttered. "Kenzie's stalker is a *woman*."

And I had no doubt in my mind she was working with Alan. She clearly had a connection to him, visiting as regularly as she did. While he'd been locked up on the inside, she was out and about, free to do whatever she could to attack Kenzie.

"Call Charlie and update him about this," Daniel told Jude, who was already on the phone making that call.

Jada Moyer might be a woman, but that didn't mean she was any less deadly to Kenzie.

Chapter Twenty-Six

Kenzie

For the second occasion in too short of a time frame, I woke in the back seat of a car. When I'd been hit with the stun gun, all I could do was ride out the jolt of pain. It left me numb and unable to fight back when the tall man approached and jabbed another needle into my arm. I vaguely recalled the woman giving Baldie the order to shut me up. Shut me up. Ha. I hadn't even opened my mouth long enough to ask what the hell was going on before I was zapped.

I didn't delay opening my eyes this time. Why bother, when I'd already seen the two thugs and the woman who'd approached? I was in a different car now. It was roomier and had that new-car smell. Only the woman was in the car, driving. The two goons were absent, and I wasn't sure if that was good or bad news.

I blinked, trying to refocus on being awake again after being forced to sleep. Fuzziness filled my mind, and my mouth felt dry and desperate for water after whatever they'd injected me with twice now. I definitely wasn't functioning at one hundred percent.

All I could do was rock with the motion of the car in the dark. No lights around, no moon's reflection anymore, just darkness.

I narrowed my eyes at the back of the woman's head, still

trying to place her exactly from her hair and the slim rectangle view of her face that I could see in the rearview mirror.

She'd been to one of my workshops. But why would I remember her? I met literally hundreds of people who'd attended my workshops.

The woman sighed, an, annoyed sound, and it hit me.

This woman hadn't been to just one of my workshops; she'd been to at least *two*. That's why I remembered her. She'd asked questions—always tagging that sigh to the end of them.

Jennifer?

Janelle?

That was close, but not right. I grimaced, racking my tired brain to dig deep and think hard.

Jada?

Jada. Yes, her name was Jada something.

Her eyes met mine in the rearview mirror. "You're awake."

That same damned sigh was attached to the end of her statement.

"I remember you." My words came out rough and mushy. My mouth wasn't working right. "You've come to a couple of my workshops. Your name is Jada, right?"

"You do remember. I'm a little impressed. I've actually been to four of your precious workshops." Another annoying sigh.

"What the hell is going on, Jada?"

"Now, now. No need for that tone. There's no reason we can't be civilized."

I squirmed, testing to see if my hands were any looser in the bindings. They weren't. "Civilized? You hire thugs to kidnap me, and you want to talk about being friendly?"

She shook her head. "You're not usually this snarky."

I rolled my eyes. "You'll have to excuse me if being drugged and kidnapped makes me a little testy."

She shrugged. "Couldn't be helped."

"What is going on?" I hated the anxiety that snuck into my tone. I didn't want this woman to hear my fear.

But she still picked up on it. "There's no need to be afraid."

I narrowed my eyes at her. "Forgive me for not believing you on that claim."

"I don't want to hurt you."

"That would be more convincing if you hadn't hired thugs to kidnap me and knock me out."

And Jensen. I had to cling to the hope that he was okay. I wouldn't be able to function otherwise.

"Seriously, I don't have any intention of hurting you." She sighed again. "I just want you out of the way. I need you to be far, far away. Everything I've done has been working toward that."

Holy shit. "You're my stalker?"

She shrugged. "Let's just say I'm the one who organized the stalking events. You're not the only person who's good at multi-tasking."

I shook my head, trying to get rid of the fuzziness. "What?"

"The parts I could do—the notes, the messages, even the animal blood in your house—I did. The other stuff...I hired out."

"Hired out," I parroted.

"You know, the physical stuff. Knocking you down in that parking lot a couple months ago. Taking you from the cabin tonight. Tampering with your car. I wasn't capable of doing those things myself, so I hired it out."

I didn't even know what to say.

"And some of the technical stuff. Finding out you were in Garnet Bend and where your boyfriend's cabin was. I have some basic computer experience, but not for stuff like that, so I paid someone else. Actually, I learned that from you."

I felt like I was Alice falling down the rabbit hole. "From me?"

"At one of your workshops, you mentioned hiring out menial

labor so that you could spend your time focusing on what was important. So that's what I did."

Stalking and kidnapping as menial labor. It sounded so reasonable coming from her lips.

Which made this all the more terrifying. I tested the zip ties at my wrists again, wincing as the bindings dug into my raw flesh.

"Why are you doing this? If I did something to offend you, I promise that was never my intention."

"No, no. If anything, I respect you." She met my eyes in the rearview mirror. "I admit, after the first one, I came to your workshops more for research about you. But each time, I learned something. You're such a gifted teacher."

Great. I'd somehow taught this woman everything she knew about stalking and kidnapping.

"But why are you doing this?"

I watched her face in the mirror as a soft smile came over her lips. "Because I love my man, and I'll do whatever I have to do to make sure we make it."

"Your man?" I asked, but I had a sickening feeling I already knew.

"Alan Ard. I know you have to remember him."

I knew it. I knew Alan had been behind all this somehow.

"I remember his fist crashing into my face and him throwing me into a wall so hard it dislocated my shoulder two years ago. He's in prison, you know."

That sigh again. "Of course I know. That's where I met him when I went to visit my brother. But what happened to you was a misunderstanding. Alan freely admits he lost his temper. But he's different now. He's changed."

What happened to me. She made it sound like I'd tripped on an uneven piece of carpet. Nothing had *happened* to me. Alan had attacked me, and I had been sure to press charges.

"He's abusive, petty, and a bully. That's a bad combination, Jada. You should stay away from him."

"You don't know him at all anymore!" Her scream caught me off guard, and I sank back against the seat. "He's changed. He's different now. But he talks about you enough that I know he's not over you. If you would just leave us alone, he and I would be fine!"

I took a breath, trying to regroup. Jada was unstable. I needed to handle this with as much care as possible, no matter how I felt about Alan.

"You're absolutely right. I see that now. But I promise you, I have no intention of getting back together with Alan *ever*. You guys make a much better couple than he and I ever did."

Especially given how they were both psychotic.

She seemed to relax a little. "I know. But you're still on his mind. So, I need you out of the picture, far away. I need you to never come back to Colorado. That way, he and I can have a fair chance at a normal life. He can build up his reputation as a Realtor again, without you holding him back like you were before."

"Okay. Consider it done." I had to grit my teeth between words, but I would tell this woman anything to get out of this in one piece. "I'll leave Colorado for good. Never see or talk to Alan again so that you two get the happily ever after you deserve."

Jada glanced at me. "Oh, come on. That's not possible. You're too big. You're too established in the industry. Truly, I respect what you've done, but because you've been so successful with all of it, there's no way you can just step back. But soon as you're out of the picture, Alan can have a chance at the life he deserves. With me."

I sucked in a breath. "Out of the picture?"

"Oh!" Jada smiled. "Not like that. I don't want to hurt you. Definitely don't want to kill you."

"It didn't feel that way when you put a rattlesnake in my tub and locked me in my bathroom."

Jada shook her head quickly. "Well, first of all, again, outsourced. I didn't do it myself. But that snake wasn't actually venomous. I got it from a breeder who removes venom. It's called venomoid surgery."

I did not give a flying fuck what the sick surgery was called. I pressed my lips together to keep from stating that.

"A bite would've hurt, but it wouldn't have killed you. I was just trying to scare you. To spook you into running like I told you to. Alan and I can't move from Colorado because of his parole issues. But I was hoping you'd just leave and start a new career somewhere far away." Another sigh. "Wishful thinking on my part —I finally figured that out."

I was trying to wrap my head around her plan since no part of it seemed to be steeped in logic.

She wanted a life with Alan but felt like my presence in Colorado was keeping them from having that. All the crazy stalking stuff hadn't been because she was obsessed or angry with me; it was because she'd wanted me to leave.

It was why she hadn't killed me, like Jensen and the Resting Warrior guys had pointed out. Killing me had never been her endgame. If she'd wanted me dead, it would've already happened.

So what the hell was she doing now? Driving me out of the country? She had to know it wouldn't stop me from coming back and pressing charges. Although I'd happily lie to convince her that wasn't true if it got me out of this.

"Where are you taking me?" I asked as calmly as I could manage. "What do you plan to do with me?"

"Well, I know this is going to seem farfetched..." she said.

Now I let out a sigh. *More fucking farfetched than this situation already was?* Difficult to believe.

"I outsourced one more time. My brother—the same one who

is in prison with Alan, so this kind of brings the entire situation in a nice full circle—has connections with some people who have developed a black-market memory drug."

I blinked. Once, twice. I'd been wrong. This was definitely more farfetched.

"Memory drug?" I asked, not liking any single syllable of what Jada said.

Once again, I looked out the window, wondering if I could survive a jump. Definitely not at this speed.

"Yes. I've thought this through, and it's the best possible plan. The drug will pretty much wipe your memory—you won't remember who you are or any part of your life."

"Jada..."

"But you won't be hurt, you see? I'll drive you really far away from Colorado, maybe Florida or something. Don't worry, I'll make sure you're safe and okay. Then I'll inject you. You won't remember anything about your past, so you'll just rebuild a new future. You'll be fine!"

It was obvious she'd spent a lot of time thinking about this and convincing herself that her words were true.

"The effects of the drugs might wear off after a few years, but that won't matter, because once you're gone, Alan will move on. With me. And when he realizes how happy he can be without you in his life, then it won't make a difference if you eventually come back."

I couldn't even figure out what to say.

"There is a chance it could permanently affect brain function." One more sigh. "But I have to try this. For Alan's sake. He deserves a full life without any hangups about you. He'll get out next week, and this is the best gift I can give him. He's worth it."

"Listen." I shook my head, frantic to make Jada see reason. "Jada, no. This is not what you want to do. This is not how you want to start your life with him."

"Kenzie, I trust my gut. Another thing you taught us in your seminar, remember? Working out what we feel is right in our gut."

Jesus fucking Christ. She'd taken every single thing I'd said and twisted it to suit her own purposes.

"But you'll never—"

The blaring ringtone of a phone cut off my next words. With the sound, the dashboard lit up.

"It's an unknown number." She shifted in her seat. "You have to be quiet now, or else I'll hang up and inject you again so you're unconscious for the rest of the trip."

"I'll be quiet." The lie slipped easily from my tongue as I thought about what I could yell to get help from whoever was calling. I'd only have a few seconds before she would hang up. Maybe my name? That I'd been kidnapped? Maybe mention Resting Warrior?

She cleared her throat and shot me a stern look before answering. "This is Jada."

"There's the voice of the woman I love."

Alan. Shit. No help to be gained there.

"Alan!" Jada squealed. "Hey, baby. How are you calling me right now?"

"I'm so glad I could reach you, my precious queen," he crooned in that falsely sweet tone he used to use with me. "I have good news."

"Yeah? What news, sweetie." Jada sat up straighter, so giddy and enthusiastic to be able to talk to him. She clearly clung to his every word. "What is it?"

"I got out a little earlier than expected."

She gasped then squealed again in excitement. "Early? You're already out now? That's how you're calling me!"

"Sure am. I can't wait to see you."

She took her hands off the wheel to clap for a second. "Where are you? I thought I was going to pick you up."

"Well, once I got out, I headed to Denver. I went by Kenzie's apartment. You know, for closure. But she wasn't there. Her neighbor told me that Kenzie hadn't been around for a while. Weird, huh?"

Wait.

He didn't know I wasn't in Denver? Jada must not have told him what she was doing. She'd been working on her own.

"Why did you need to see Kenzie?" Some of the giddiness was gone from her voice. "I thought you said you wanted to get over her."

"For closure, baby, like I said. I just feel like if I could see her one more time, then I could leave her behind me forever. Just one more time. That's all I need. To *settle* things."

Could she not hear the menace fairly dripping from his words? Yeah, he wanted to see me one more time—but not to shake my hand so we could go our separate ways.

He wanted revenge on me for putting him in jail.

"You really feel like you need to see her one more time?"

"Yes, baby. For us. To give us a clean slate to start from. But I'm afraid no one is going to understand that if I'm looking for her, you know? So, maybe you can help me. For us. Would you do that for us?"

That gaslighting son of a bitch.

Jada giggled again. "I can do us one better."

"Oh yeah? What's that?" I could tell his voice was a little colder, but Jada didn't seem to notice.

"I can bring Kenzie to you right now."

"Oh yeah, my queen." All coldness was gone from his voice now that Jada was being compliant. "You know where she is? Why don't you tell me, and I'll pay Kenzie a little visit and get this over with."

"I have her in the car with me right now."

Silence lingered for a long moment. "Right now?"

"Yep. I talked her into leaving Colorado." Her eyes met mine in the mirror, and she put a finger up to her lips, signaling me to be quiet. "I was going to help her get set up somewhere else before you got out."

More silence.

"Alan?"

"I'm just trying to wrap my head around all this. Where are you right now?"

"We're in Wyoming, coming from Montana. We were headed to Florida."

His voice turned pouty. "I can't go to Florida. I can't leave the state."

"How about if I stop by my cabin north of Denver? You won't have to violate your parole by meeting us there. We can't take a chance on anything that will land you back in jail. If seeing her one last time is what you need, we can do that. Closure, like you said."

"You're amazing, Jada. That would be perfect. I love that your cabin is in the middle of nowhere."

Her sigh was much softer this time. "I love that you found it for me to buy."

"I'm so glad I met you, my queen," he praised, laying it on thick. "I live for you, Jada. Only you."

Jada giggled, smiling shyly.

"And you're my king, handsome man. I love you so much."

I wanted to gag at all the gooey mush. Jada was eating it all up, and I knew nothing I could say would make her change her mind about what Alan claimed.

I remembered how it felt so long ago before things went sour between us. Early on in our relationship, Alan was extravagant with his affection for me too, but then it quickly sounded so fake, just like it did now.

Nothing at all like Jensen. The man called me *City* as his term of affection, for God's sake. Nothing about him would ever be considered extravagant. But he was so much more real than Alan had ever been. So much more of a man.

Tears stung my eyes. I prayed Jensen was all right. That he'd somehow gotten himself help. I couldn't stand the thought of anything else.

Promising to see Alan in just a couple of hours, Jada disconnected the call.

"Don't you worry, Kenzie. It's all going to work out. You're so smart and talented that even after the memory-loss drug, you'll still land on your feet, I'm sure of it. Let's get Alan his closure, and we'll all move on with our lives."

I tuned the other woman out. I wasn't going to be able to talk any sense into her. She was determined to bring me to the man who'd attacked me so brutally, then take me somewhere and wipe my whole life away.

All in the name of love.

Chapter Twenty-Seven

Kenzie

We arrived at Jada's cabin in the predawn hours. I had no clue what time it actually was, but I knew that my mind and body were giving in to exhaustion.

I'd tried the best I could to make Jada see any sort of reason, but she was convinced that Alan just wanted to give me one last hug goodbye and send me on my way.

I'd tried to tell her about my parents and friends, even about Jensen. Tried to explain to her how much it would hurt them if I just suddenly disappeared—which was what would happen if she went through with this insane memory-drug plan.

Her response just solidified how much of fairy tale she was living in.

"No, don't think of it that way. Think of it as the perfect solution. That we all get to have our happily ever after."

Jada was not interested in reality.

"Here we are!" She put the car in park and clapped her hands. "I can't believe I finally get to see Alan with no guard standing watch over us. I can touch him and hold him as much as I want. That's not going to be hard for you, right?"

She was talking to me like we were girlfriends. Like I was some awkward third wheel. I didn't bother to answer.

She rushed around to open the door for me and yank me out of the car when I didn't move fast enough. She hustled us up the stairs to the small cabin in the middle of nowhere.

The cabin Alan had found for her. I'd thought about that a lot the past few hours. Maybe Jada hadn't been honest with Alan about what she had planned for me, but I was pretty damn certain he hadn't been honest about what he'd planned for this place.

But I was sure it included me not leaving here alive.

"He's just inside," she reminded me excitedly, almost like a hyper Chihuahua.

When we walked inside, she squealed and ran to him, her arms wide open. "Alan!"

Even though he stood hugging Jada to his side, his eyes were locked on me and promising retribution.

I was definitely not leaving this place alive if he had anything to say about it.

I wasn't going to wait around to see if my theory was true.

I turned to run, willing to take my chances in my slippers and with my hands tied, but I stopped when I spotted two men standing by the door, blocking it.

Both of them looked me over from head to toe, demented smiles finding their faces but not reaching their cold, dead eyes. I had no doubt Alan had brought these two particular men here for a reason. They both fairly oozed a hunger for violence.

Jada was too wrapped up in kissing all over Alan to have even noticed them yet.

Or to have even noticed that Alan's attention was more on me than her.

Ignoring the pain, I continued to work on the zip tie that bound my hands, trying my best not to draw any attention to my motions. My raw skin was bloody now, but I didn't care. If I had any hope of making it out of here alive, I was going to need my hands. And I was quite certain bloody wrists were about to become the least of my worries.

"See, baby?" Jada finally pulled back from kissing Alan. "I brought her just like I said I would."

She turned, her bright smile fading when she saw the two men by the door. "What's going on, Alan? Who are these guys?"

"I just wanted to make sure we were safe, so I brought a few guys with me."

A few. I could be wrong, but that might mean there were more of his goons outside.

Jada laughed nervously. "I don't think that was necessary. I mean, what is she going to do? Plus, I'm not comfortable with them just staring at us. Can't you send them home?"

Alan looked down at Jada and gave her an indulgent smile. "How about if I send them outside?"

She obviously didn't like that as much, but she nodded. "Okay."

Alan gestured toward the door with his head, and the two men left without a word. He crossed his arms over his chest, giving me a once-over before locking his eyes on mine.

"Now you can say whatever you need to get off your chest." Jada followed, patting him on the back in support. "You can tell her goodbye. Good riddance. Whatever has been bugging you—"

He shook off her hand and walked forward until he got right up in my face. "We meet again, Mackenzie."

God, in light of all the other shitty things he'd done, I'd totally forgotten his penchant for calling me by my full name, even though nobody else—not even my own parents—ever had.

So pretentious. So Alan.

What a dick.

I remained perfectly still, not that there was much I could do to ward off a blow if it was coming. But I wouldn't give him the satisfaction of knowing how scared I was, despite the anger and hatred pulsing from him like a living, breathing thing.

"Do you know what I lost because of you?"

I refused to reply. I knew he didn't really want me to. He wanted to remind me that he was the one with the power. That he was the one calling the shots.

"I've dreamed of this day." Each word was more forceful than the last.

"Of course you have!" Jada rushed up to us. She was still trying to hold on to her chipper attitude, but I could see the hesitation, the worry in her eyes she tried to hide. "We've been counting down to your release day for so long. And now that it's here, we can start the rest of our lives together."

Alan didn't acknowledge her words or reply. But he did pull out a knife and wave it in front of my face before thrusting it under my chin. I winced as the tip drew blood.

"I've waited a long time to give you what you deserve for putting me behind bars, you bitch."

"Alan?" Jada's eyes went wide at the sight of the knife in my face, and her voice shook with fear. "No. Alan, no! What are you doing?"

"Paying her back," he bit out in a growl. His evil gaze remained locked on me as he fumed. His nostrils flared. The skin below his right eye twitched.

Jada grabbed his arm. "Sweetheart, wait. I know you're angry, but it doesn't need to be like this. I have a plan to get her out of your life—out of *our* lives—for good."

"Yeah, you told me. You convinced her to go to Florida."

"But it's more than that. You know that memory-altering drug my brother talks about? I've got some. Once she's in Florida, I'll inject her with a crazy-high dose, and she won't remember who she is or who you are or anything."

He lowered the knife and looked over at her. "You have some of the drug?"

Jada's smile widened now that he was paying attention to her.

"Yep." She pulled both the stun gun and two syringes out of her small handbag. "Stun gun helped me get her here. And this compound will help me get rid of her for good."

He picked up one of the syringes and studied it. "So she won't have any memory of anything once she's injected?"

"Nope." She reached up on her tiptoes and kissed him on the cheek. "She'll be out of our lives for good. You can rebuild your real estate career, just like we planned."

He took the stun gun from her other hand. "And you used this to subdue her?"

Jada beamed, watching as he flipped it on and off multiple times. "Yep. I remember how you told me weapons are our friends."

I braced myself to get stunned again. I knew by the light in Alan's eyes that he was looking forward to causing me pain. I couldn't stop my breath from catching as he looked over at me and smiled.

But he turned the stun gun on Jada instead. I winced, watching her shake and jerk while he held the device on her much longer than she had on me. She fell to the floor, moaning even after he stopped.

"She'll never understand that she means fucking nothing to me." He pushed at her with his foot, rolling her over to the side. I had no idea if she was conscious or not, as still as she was. "She was always sighing, always dramatic. Clingy and wanting to fix things. She was a helpful means to an end."

He smiled at me once more, stepping closer while I fought with the zip tie at my wrists. "But she bought this nice, secluded cabin just because we talked about it. Lots of space here, don't you think? Nobody around for miles. Plenty of places to hide a body where it will never be found."

I tried to keep my features blank and think of anything to stall while I quietly worked on the bindings.

I knew Alan was going to kill me. In his eyes, it would be perfectly justifiable revenge for ruining his life.

He set down the stun gun and syringes on the table but still wielded the knife in his hand, slicing it in the air and jabbing it toward me like he couldn't decide where to start. I knew whatever action he took toward me was going to hurt. His eyes were lit with excitement at the thought.

"Nothing to say?" He smirked. "Not going to beg me to let you go, let you live? Apologize for ruining my life the way you did so many times?"

He'd never been able to take responsibility for his own actions. Even before the night he'd attacked me, he'd always tried to make every setback or failure my fault. He'd accused me of making him lose his job, making him get mad, and so much more.

"Always my fault, wasn't it?" I managed to get out, my voice stronger than I'd thought it would be.

"You never thought about me? Never thought about how you ruined my damn life? Just because we had a little argument."

"You assaulted me," I argued. The dark look in his eyes scared me. I needed to try to talk him down, not antagonize him more. "You were done with me, Alan. Even before that night you attacked me, we were done. You're out of jail. This can all be behind you. There's no need for us to be here at all."

"Except payback." He lifted the knife again, and I took a cowardly step back before I could think about it. I didn't want to be boxed into a corner, but it looked like that's where Alan was directing me. I'd have no chance to try to run if he maneuvered me there.

"Just let me go."

He sucked in a deep breath, obviously savoring what was about to happen.

My time was up.

The knife was coming at me in a slicing motion, when out of the blue, Jada wobbled into him. I hadn't even realized she'd gotten off the floor.

"No!" Her voice was filled with pain as she jumped on his back and tried to pull him away from me. She ripped at his hair and face.

"Don't, Alan. You don't need to hurt her! That wasn't the plan. Nobody needs to get hurt!"

"I'm not going to hurt her. I'm going to fucking kill her!"

Jada fought harder, despite Alan now slicing the knife at her. The two of them fell into the table. Alan's two men from outside ran in and rushed over to pull Jada off Alan.

"Give me a syringe, now!" Alan demanded, pointing to where one had rolled onto the floor. One of the men grabbed it and handed it to Alan. He didn't wait a second more as he uncapped the needle and jabbed it into Jada's skin.

She screamed, trying to pull away from the sting, but Alan pushed the plunger in all the way.

He grabbed her chin. "Now you can move on too, bitch. You can move on to not even remembering who the hell I am. And this means I don't need to worry about a witness for what I'm about to do to Mackenzie."

Jada crumpled to the floor. Did it kill her? Cause her to pass out? I didn't know.

All I knew was that poor Jada's demise was the opportunity I'd been waiting for.

I yanked again at the zip tie binding my wrists, giddy to find it finally loose enough that I could slip my hands out. I didn't linger for a second. I turned and took off as fast as I could toward the door.

Both my slippers fell off, but I couldn't stop for them. I would have to go barefoot.

I knew an attack had to be coming. Alan had a knife, the other two had guns. I braced for agony in my back at any moment.

"No! Don't shoot. I will be the one to kill her, and I'm going to do it slow."

I heard Alan's angry shouts and heavy footfalls behind me as I dashed toward the trees. If Alan wanted to be the one to kill me, I would take it since it gave me more time.

I had never been much of a runner, and running barefoot didn't help. I shut off my mind and pushed every ounce of strength into my legs. I weaved through the trees, going left and right, hoping to confuse the men following me. I was also hoping to prevent them from having a good target to shoot me in the back, despite Alan's words that he'd be the only one to kill me.

There was little moonlight, so it was difficult to see exactly where I was going. I tried to stay as quiet as possible, but my heavy breaths still echoed in the silence. I was tiring fast and slowing down. When I tripped and caught myself against a tree, I knew I was in trouble.

"You've got five of us looking for you, Mackenzie," Alan taunted. "You didn't know that I had two other men keeping watch out here, did you?"

I didn't reply to give myself away, but I was pretty sure his voice came from the left. I turned right and put on a burst of speed. I knew I had to keep running.

If I stopped, I died.

"I'm going to take my sweet time carving you up, Mackenzie. You know that?"

I fisted my hands and turned left between a cluster of trees. I was hearing sounds and voices all around now. I knew they were closing in and surrounding me.

"I spent months fantasizing about how sweetly you'll cry and beg for me to spare your life."

I held back a whimper at his mocking tone. A hard step down on a branch caused me to stumble and bite my tongue to keep from crying out in pain.

"But I won't!" he yelled. "I won't spare you a damn thing, bitch. You're going to die screaming."

I had to stop, the pain in my foot throbbing. I rounded a thick tree trunk and paused to catch my breath. I felt a sticky substance on the bottom of my foot and realized I had cut it. I was bleeding.

Great. Now I was leaving a trail for them to follow from that damn branch.

I heaved in a huge breath and staggered to fully standing and darted off in the opposite direction. Before I made it more than a few steps, a callused hand clapped over my mouth.

I couldn't believe Alan had found me so quickly. A few seconds ago, he'd sounded farther away.

I strained, bucking and kicking and twisting to get free. I couldn't let him win, couldn't give up.

Then all of a sudden, I smelled it. Past the fear, the sound of my heart pounding in my ears, my ragged breath.

Smelled *him*. Clean spruce and mechanical grease.

All man. And all Jensen.

He was alive, and he was here. He'd kept his promise and had come to protect me just like he'd vowed he would.

All the fight suddenly went out of me, and I sank into his warm embrace.

He wrapped his arms around me, pulling me firmly back against his chest, hugging me tight. Jensen had come for me.

He was here.

Chapter Twenty-Eight

Jensen

I had never felt such relief as having Kenzie in my arms.

She was alive.

She breathed hard as she collapsed back against me. Her chest heaved up and down harshly as she sucked in air.

All I could do was relish holding her in my arms. But only for a second. We weren't out of this yet.

Ever since we'd learned about the threats Alan had been voicing toward her in jail, I'd feared the worst. I was afraid we'd be too late.

And we almost had been. She was out here running from five men barefoot, for Christ's sake. She wouldn't have lasted much longer.

I owed Ian DeRose, the owner of Zodiac Tactical, a man I'd only met briefly, everything I owned and then some.

When we'd found out Jada Moyer had bought a secluded cabin based on emails Alan had sent her, we knew this had to be where they were taking Kenzie. We hadn't had enough proof for local law enforcement to be willing to send someone all the way out here. Plus, we'd known that could quickly get botched—a cop coming in lights blazing might've caused Alan to do something deadly.

Ian had offered his private jet, and a few hours later, we'd been here.

Not a moment too soon.

Kenzie was alive and back in my arms. I refused to think about ever letting her go again.

"Jensen." She gripped my cheeks, her voice choppy and stuttering with the violent shivers that racked her body between the cold and the adrenaline. "You're alive. I didn't know... I didn't... I was so worried..."

I kissed her softly. "Me too, City. But be quiet now. We're not out of danger."

I slipped off my jacket and wrapped it around her then picked her up. She was barefoot, and it was freezing out. "Are you hurt?"

"Just c-cold. And I cut my foot."

I wasn't so worried about the cut, but with these temps and what little she was wearing, even in my jacket, hypothermia was a real concern. Not to mention she was going to cool down quickly now that she wasn't running for her life. I set her down on a log behind a large tree. It was as secluded as we were going to get.

I pressed the comms earpiece. "I've got Kenzie. Fast movement is not much of an option."

"Roger," Lucas responded. "Keep her hidden. Some of these guys are trained."

By trained, Lucas probably meant former military. But it definitely meant they knew what they were doing, hunting people out in the wilderness in the dim light of barely dawn.

"I wish we had the rest of the team here," Daniel muttered. "I'm moving around the south side of the cabin."

The Resting Warrior team was spread thin. Everyone had been off following different leads, doing what they could to find Kenzie. Lucas, Daniel, and I had been the only ones close enough to make the Zodiac Tactical jet when it arrived at the nearby regional airport.

"We'll head that way too, Jensen," Lucas added. "Try to lead everyone away from you guys. Hunter?"

"Roger."

Oh yeah, and we had Lucas's cousin. Dude was even quieter than me—I wasn't sure I'd heard him speak a whole sentence yet. I didn't know anything about him or even why he'd shown up in Garnet Bend, but he'd been willing to help, and that was enough for me. Especially since he was former Special Forces.

Kenzie was pulling at my arm. "You guys have to be careful. They're armed. And Alan is out for blood."

Every once in a while, Alan yelled out some threat, obviously trying to intimidate Kenzie.

"As long as he's running his mouth, he's giving us an advantage. Letting us know exactly where he is." I kept my voice low, just slightly louder than a whisper. A whisper actually carried farther to others than a consistently low tone. "It's the quiet guys he's hired we have to worry about."

"One man down." Hunter's voice came through my ear. I wasn't sure exactly what *down* meant coming from him. "Southeast side of the cabin."

Apparently, Daniel wasn't sure what Hunter meant either. "Let's try to keep the body count to a minimum, if possible."

"Affirmative," Hunter replied.

That still didn't tell us if he'd killed anybody or not. But honestly, I didn't care. The only thing I cared about was getting Kenzie out of this safely. If some bad guys didn't survive, that was their own problem.

But just as I'd feared, shudders were racking Kenzie's body. She was slumping over against me, her system shutting down. I ripped off my black beanie and pushed it down onto her head before pulling her as close to my body as I could.

I was no medic, but I knew enough about survival situations to know we were fighting a losing battle as long as she was out in the elements. She was losing heat from too many sources, plus her body was already run down from lack of sleep and God knew what else.

I sat next to her and pulled off my boots and socks, then crouched down to put them on Kenzie.

"N-no." She tried to push my hands away. "You need them."

I cupped her cheeks and put my face right in front of hers. "This is not just me flirting, okay? I'm not being gallant. We need to get you warm if we want to get out of this alive."

"But—"

"City, I need you to trust me." We didn't have time to debate this.

She nodded. "I do. I do trust you, Jensen. Tell me what to do."

Her trust meant everything to me.

I took the socks and boots and put them on her feet. The boots would hardly stay on, even with the ankles laced up as tight as they could go. But it at least meant she wasn't leaking heat from either her feet or head now. That would mitigate at least some of what she was up against physically.

"You have to be cold, Mackenzie," Alan called out, much closer than I would like him to be. "You can't survive out here on your own, dressed like you are. Come back to the cabin, and we can talk. I lost my temper. You always make me lose my temper."

"Then get some self-restraint, asshole," she muttered.

I grabbed her hand and pulled her in the opposite direction from the cabin. I did my best to ignore the biting pain shooting through my feet from the cold, but without my hat and jacket, it wouldn't be long before I was the one in trouble.

We would have to deal with that when we came to it. Right now, Kenzie was in the more dire shape of the two of us.

Keeping her hand in mine, I moved us as quietly as I could

through the trees. Her lack of energy, combined with the boots that were much too large for her, caused her to keep stumbling. She would've fallen multiple times if I hadn't had hold of her.

"Another down." Hunter spoke again.

But again, no definition of what down meant.

"Going off comms," Hunter said, slightly out of breath, as if he was running.

"Hunter, no. Stay on comms." Daniel was the team leader. The guys listened to him.

But Hunter wasn't on the normal Resting Warrior team. And evidently, he had already disconnected his communications unit.

"Fuck," Daniel said. "Lucas."

"On it." Lucas's voice was breathier now too. He was also running.

I couldn't worry about family politics at the moment. Hunter was on our side, and that was all I cared about.

I cursed as a rain/snow mix started to fall. Conditions were deteriorating, which could be deadlier than the men with the guns if we weren't careful.

"I'm moving Kenzie to the vehicle. Body temp is critical."

I wasn't sure if I was talking about hers or mine, but it didn't matter because we were both in trouble.

"Roger." Lucas was obviously still running by the sound of his breathing.

"Roger that," Daniel said. "We'll handle things here."

We'd parked the car about three miles away and had come in on foot in order to make sure we were not detected. Now, I wished we had just barreled in hot.

Kenzie stumbled again. I wrapped my arm more tightly around her waist, trying to take as much of her weight as I could to help her. "Hang in there, City. You're doing great."

She didn't answer. Her feet were dragging more with each step. We were going to be in real trouble soon.

And we hadn't heard anything from Alan in way too long. That did not reassure me. The only reason I could think of that he would stop taunting Kenzie was if he was up to something.

Or maybe he was the second man Hunter had taken down—hopefully permanently. I wouldn't lose a bit of sleep over that.

But either way, I pulled my Glock from its holster and kept it low at my side. Kenzie and I were making way too much noise not to be tracked if anyone was nearby.

We made it another half mile at a pace way too slow before I lost feeling in my feet. Just trying to keep us both upright was getting more and more difficult. Kenzie stumbled again, and I started to estimate how far I could carry her. Although I already knew the answer.

I would carry her however fucking far I had to.

There was no way I was leaving her. We would walk as far as we could, and then I would manage from—

The tackle caught me completely unaware. My gun flew in one direction, and I pushed Kenzie in the other.

"She's not worth it, you know." Alan's words penetrated my brain right before his fist connected with my jaw. He got in two more punches to my gut before I could react and roll to the side.

"I have to admit, I didn't think Mackenzie was going to have her own rescue party here. Good thing I brought super soldiers of my own. How about if we let my guys take care of your guys? I don't think it will be a problem for me to get rid of you."

I didn't wait for Ard to pull up his weapon and point it at me —I dove for him from my half-crouched position on the ground, knocking his gun from his hand.

I trained with the Resting Warrior guys on a regular basis, so my hand-to-hand combat skills were pretty finely honed. But the time in the cold with inadequate clothing was taking its toll. I was clumsy and slower to react than normal.

When he pulled out a knife, I knew I was in trouble. Even more so when one of his guys stepped out into our small clearing.

Once again, I didn't hesitate to jump for the tackle. If the man had a chance to get his weapon up, it was all over for me and Kenzie. He was bigger than Alan, but I focused and used as much agility as I could muster. I would only have one chance to neutralize him as a threat. If I allowed him to get up, I'd be fighting a battle on two fronts.

And I'd lose.

I got in two punches to the gut while the guy was still stunned by the tackle. A third one had him winded enough that I was able to hop to my feet and grab the guy by the collar of his jacket. I put every bit of strength into my haymaker punch. It knocked him out cold.

But before I could turn around to face Alan, he had the tip of his knife at my throat. "Not so fast, lover boy."

"I'm not here alone, Ard. Your men are being taken out one by one, and then you'll go down too."

"Maybe. Maybe not." His voice was smug. "But I'm afraid you won't be here to witness that."

"Fuck off, you coward."

"Look at you. No coat, no shoes. You gave them to Mackenzie, didn't you? What a Boy Scout."

I shifted my weight slightly, ready to spin and try to take him down. But he wasn't falling for that again.

"Nuh-uh-uh." He pressed the knife into my neck. I could feel the tip piercing my skin, blood starting to flow. It stopped my movement. "If you'd kept your stuff, maybe you'd be in better shape to fight."

But then Kenzie would be dead or close to it by now. That hadn't even been an option.

"And look," Alan continued, "all for nothing. That selfish bitch ran off to save herself."

As the knife slid into my neck even farther, I couldn't feel anything but relief that Kenzie had run. I wouldn't make it, but hopefully she would. That was all that mattered.

"Mackenzie!" Alan yelled. "If you care about your friend at all, you'll come back here."

"Don't do it, City!" No matter what Alan did, I didn't want her coming back here.

But I couldn't stop myself from crying out when Alan slammed his knife into my shoulder. The pain and motion of it forced me down to my knees.

"Do you want him to die, Mackenzie?"

"He'll kill me anyway!" I knew that much was true, but the words got me another burning stab from the fucker.

"I don't think she's coming for you," he said as I attempted to breathe through the pain and gather what remaining strength I had. "I thought she had feelings for you, but I guess I was wrong."

"Or maybe she's just too smart to fall for your bullshit."

"I tell you what. Let's try a different route."

I expected another stab, prepped myself not to let out a sound, but it didn't come.

"Maybe I won't kill him, Mackenzie. Look what I've got— Jada's little memory drug. How about we make sure that even if he survives, he never remembers anything about you."

What the fuck? I had no idea what drug he was talking about, but I knew he wasn't bluffing. I could see the syringe in his other hand.

There was no way I was letting him inject me with that stuff, but I knew I was down to my last reserves of strength. I couldn't feel my feet at all, and the rest of my body wasn't in much better shape. That stab with the knife had pretty much rendered my left arm useless.

The guys would hear all the yelling and be on their way. They wouldn't be able to help me, but maybe I could buy some time for them to help Kenzie.

"See?" Alan leaned close to my ear and lowered his volume. "I keep trying to tell everyone what a bitch she is, but nobody believes me. She left you to save herself, and now you're going to pay the price."

"Fuck. You." My voice sounded weak even to my own ears.

"I'm going to finish what I started with her. She's not going to live to tattle on me again."

I waited for the knife or the syringe, but neither came. Instead, Alan cried out in pain then crashed to the ground beside me, holding his head.

Kenzie swung the large branch at him again, striking him on the head, causing him to fall flat, completely out. "I don't think so, asshole. You're never going to lay your hands on me again."

She dropped the heavy branch and rushed over to put her arms around me.

"You didn't leave me," I managed to mutter. The world was going in and out of focus.

"Never."

It was the last thing I heard as I slumped to the ground.

Chapter Twenty-Nine

Kenzie

Two months later

I stared out the window of my Denver office, a view I'd always loved. I'd leased this place three years ago because of the view of the city skyline. The office space had actually been less expensive than the ones across the hall because of that view—*not* facing the Rocky Mountains, like most people wanted. Worked great for me because I'd preferred the city view.

But not anymore. Now, I found I didn't want the city view or the mountain views.

At least not *these* mountain views.

I should be happy, not pensively staring out my window. My nightmare was over.

The police eventually arrived at the cabin that night, but by then, everything had been nearly taken care of. Lucas and Daniel had helped me get Jensen to the cabin and warm enough not to be critical. By the time the ambulance had arrived to get him to the hospital for his knife wound, he'd at least been stable.

Jensen had saved me. If he and the Resting Warrior guys

hadn't shown up when they had, if he hadn't so selflessly given me his jacket and shoes, if he hadn't fought Alan despite Alan's knife, I definitely wouldn't have made it.

Most of the night was still a blur for me, even now. From what I understood, Lucas's cousin Hunter had taken out most of Alan's hired thugs: two dead, two severely beaten. But when we got back to the cabin with Jensen, Hunter had been gone.

Jada had been too.

Evidently, disappearing was Hunter's modus operandi, according to Lucas. For years, he'd been trying to get Hunter to come stay at Resting Warrior. After all, the ranch was meant for people exactly like Hunter: a former Special Forces soldier who was having difficulty adapting back into civilian life. Hunter's demons apparently didn't give him much peace.

Lucas was certain Hunter would eventually show back up. But to keep him out of trouble with the law since he wasn't there to give a statement, Lucas and Daniel had taken responsibility for what had been done to the thugs.

Not that the police had cared overly much. Alan's guys all had extensive rap sheets and were all wanted for various crimes. Taking them out had been doing law enforcement a service, especially in a situation like this where everything was very cut-and-dried.

Except for when it came to Jada.

She'd saved my life too. Despite the stalking, and that she was obviously a little off her rocker, if she hadn't jumped on Alan when she did, I'd be dead right now.

So, the thought of her injected with that damned amnesia drug and off on her own somewhere? I didn't like it. She had to be terrified—no memory of anything about her life, no resources... I hoped they found her soon. Less for making her pay for her actions and more for getting her help. She needed it now more than ever.

Alan was heading back to prison, this time under multiple counts of attempted murder. There would be no early parole for him a second time.

My life was truly my own once again. I could see my friends and family whenever I wanted to. My seminars for the next few months were set up and almost sold out.

Everything I'd wanted when I'd rolled into Garnet Bend a few months ago, I now had. I was free to live and do whatever I wanted. Get back to the business that was so important to me.

But all I could think about was Jensen.

I'd seen him, of course. I'd stayed with him in the hospital the two days he was there, and then I had helped him get settled back at home afterward. He'd been a grumpy patient, not wanting to sit still, but I'd found ways to convince him to stay in bed.

Then the next weekend, my parents had come to meet him. They'd loved him—and Garnet Bend—like I knew they would. And, God bless Jensen, he'd eaten my mother's cooking with a smile on his face as if he couldn't taste how terrible it was.

But then it had been time for me to go back into the career I'd spent such a long time building. The career that had brought me so much joy and fulfillment.

The career that now seemed a little empty if it meant I was going to have a life without Jensen.

I loved him. He loved me. We talked multiple times every single day. But how did this work with us so far apart?

My phone buzzed on my desk, and I pressed the intercom button to answer. "Kenzie, your three o'clock is here."

Shit. I was so out of it, I hadn't even realized I had a late-afternoon appointment. I glanced at my calendar and didn't see anything written down.

"Samantha, I don't even know what appointment this is," I told my assistant. I hated being unprepared for a meeting. It wasted both my time and my client's. "It's not on my schedule."

"Sorry, boss. I must have forgotten to write it down."

I swallowed my frustration. Samantha didn't make mistakes like this very often. Never, in fact. "Maybe we should reschedule so that..."

I trailed off as Jensen walked into my office and shut the door behind him. "Samantha was covering for me. I asked her to block out some time for me on your calendar but not let you know I was coming."

I couldn't help myself. I rushed around my desk and into his arms.

I breathed him in. God, that smell. No matter how much I was near him, the scent of Jensen always felt like coming home.

"Why didn't you tell me you were coming? How long are you staying? I'm so happy to see you!"

He cupped my cheeks with his hands and drew me in for a kiss. We were both breathless by the time we pulled away.

"Maybe I can send Samantha home early," I whispered. I'd done that the last time he'd come to visit. I could hardly work at my desk anymore without remembering Jensen bending me over it.

But he shook his head. "Actually, today, I'm here as a client."

I started to chuckle, but then I realized he was serious. "Wait. Really?"

"Yes, if you have time." He pulled back slightly. "I'd like to talk about real estate."

"Well, sir, you've come to the right place." I went back to sit at my desk and gestured for him to take the chair across from it.

"I'm looking for a commercial real estate location."

Maybe he was thinking about opening a second shop in Garnet Bend, although I couldn't figure out why he'd want to do that. Regardless, I wasn't licensed as a real estate agent in Montana.

At least, not yet. I had looked into the requirements for

becoming a Realtor there. But I hadn't mentioned my research to him. After all, we hadn't made any definite plans for the future together. Even if I wanted to move to Montana—which I wasn't sure I did—I didn't know if he even wanted me there permanently.

But for right now, I would listen to him as a client and try to offer my best advice. "Well, the first step would be figuring out exactly what you need, and then we could find an agent in Montana who could help you secure that."

"Actually, I'm looking for a place in or around Denver."

I froze in the middle of grabbing my notebook so I could jot down particulars. "Denver?"

"Yes. Particularly, I'm looking for some sort of small woodshop for woodworking."

Was he saying what I thought he was saying?

"Jensen…"

"This isn't working for me, City. This being so far away from you. I love you, and I want us to figure out a way to be together."

I closed my eyes. There was nothing I wanted more than to be close to him. Jensen was it for me. He was the one I wanted to spend the rest of my life with.

And while I didn't want to leave behind the career I'd worked so hard to build, I knew I also couldn't ask him to give up the only true family he'd ever known and move here.

"I don't want you to come here." I forced the words out.

I opened my eyes to find him staring at me with a half-startled, half-concerned look on his face. "Have I misread this thing between us? Were you not thinking of us as long-term?"

I shook my head. "No, I love you and want to be with you too. The *longest* of terms. But I can't ask you to leave Garnet Bend. That's your home, your family."

"Actually, I don't plan to leave Garnet Bend, not permanently.

But I don't expect you to give up everything here to move there either."

I let out a sad sigh. "Then what do we do?"

"We do both."

Excitement had heat radiating through my chest. "How?"

"We add a room on to my cabin in Garnet Bend for the sole purpose of it becoming your second office. I will make sure we have the fastest internet available, so you can conduct business there whenever you need to."

I stood up, nodding slowly. "Go on."

"We find a place for me here so that, like I said, I can have a woodworking shop. That's bringing in a lot of my income anyway. I can hire a second mechanic for the shop, which will free me up to come here and do woodwork as much as I want."

I walked around my desk so I was leaning on it in front of him. I could literally feel my heart thundering in my chest with exhilaration. "You've put a lot of thought into this."

"You're worth a lot of thought. And even more, you're worth a lot of effort." He hooked his hands onto my hips and pulled me down to sit on his lap. "I also looked into the regional airports near Garnet Bend. Did you know one of the smaller airlines has flights to Denver and back four times a week? Airport is an hour away, but..."

"But that's very doable," I finished for him.

He nodded. "I want to make this work, City. I want you in my life, and if that means making changes to create space for you, I'm more than willing to do it."

"Me too, Jensen. I love that we're opposites, but that those opposites attract. Let's do it. Let's commit right here and now to doing whatever it takes to make this work."

He pulled me in for a kiss. "Good, because I've already talked to the town council about changing the sign. I even offered to carve a fancy one for them."

"What sign?" I asked against his lips.

"The one as you pull into town."

I remembered it from the first day. "Oh yeah? Change it to what?"

"Garnet Bend. Population 2519."

That sounded absolutely perfect to me.

Bonus Epilogue

Jensen

One year after the end of MONTANA HEAT

I stared in the mirror, putting my tie on then taking it off for the thirty-seventh time.

A tie was overkill, right? Dale and Barbara Hurst—Kenzie's parents—had never seen me in a tie. Why would I be wearing one today?

Except for the fact that I was going to attempt to convince Dale to give me his blessing to ask his daughter to marry me.

Let's face it, a tie wasn't going to disguise how I grew up or the fact that both my parents were abusive drug addicts. That wasn't exactly the bloodline someone wanted to invite into his family.

I took the tie off and threw it to the side. A tie was ridiculous anyway. Dale was coming over early while Kenzie and Barbara were out shopping together so I could show him my latest woodworking projects here in my Denver workplace.

It had taken Kenzie and I a while to find the right balance between Denver and Garnet Bend. But we'd managed because that had been the only option. Neither of us had been willing to let this relationship *not* work.

For the past few months, we'd been spending more and more time in Garnet Bend, especially once Kenzie had passed the state exam to get her licensure to become a real estate agent in Montana. She said it was a wide-open frontier—literally and figuratively—and she'd be a fool not to expand her business.

So now she mostly only came back to Colorado for her live seminars. I'd gone to one of them just to see what it was like and had been downright amazed. In front of an audience of hundreds she'd been engaging and encouraging and informative. She had such a gift and passion for helping others. Hell, her presentation had almost made me want to go into commercial real estate.

She'd also started doing a lot of personal coaching, which she could do via video chat in Garnet Bend. As promised, I'd made sure the cabin had a dedicated space just for her where she could work as much or as little as she wanted.

I'd kept a careful eye on her as we'd started spending more time in Garnet Bend. I wanted to make sure she wasn't unhappy and trying to hide it. But that hadn't been the case at all.

On any given day I'd find her having coffee with the ladies at Deja Brew or running over to Resting Warrior to help out with one thing or another. The weekly family dinners had become part of our routine.

She truly was the 2519th member of our town's population.

Maybe most surprising had been how the situation with Jada had played out, despite the woman having stalked and kidnapped Kenzie. It had gone down a road none of us would've ever dreamed—in the most exciting and heartbreaking of ways.

And Kenzie's part in that had just made me love her more.

Although I wasn't sure that was even possible. But I knew for damned sure that I had a ring that was burning a hole in my pocket.

Since we were in Denver less and less, we hadn't been seeing as much of her parents. We might not be back here for three or four more months, so I wanted to talk to Kenzie's father today.

The doorbell rang and I looked over at the tie one more time, but left it where it had landed on the sink counter and ran down to let Dale in.

He immediately noticed my collared shirt. "I thought we were doing woodshop stuff. Did I forget and we're meeting the girls somewhere?"

I was definitely glad I hadn't worn the tie. "No. I, uh, just... Laundry day."

Dale smiled as he shook my hand. "Totally understand. Good to see you."

Dale and Barbara had been nothing but totally accepting of me, each in their own way. Barbara was more like her daughter, outgoing and physically demonstrative—always hugging me or patting my hand. Dale was more reserved, his personality matching his math teacher profession, but he'd still welcomed me as Kenzie's significant other.

But what I was going to ask for today was an entirely different story. It was one thing to be okay with a guy your daughter was dating. Quite another to be okay with her tying her life to him forever.

We chatted pretty easily as we headed back to the workshop. I'd been teaching Dale how to do some basic carvings, which he'd liked. But he more enjoyed precision measuring and cutting using some of my bigger machinery, not surprising given the mathematical nature of it.

We worked for an hour, partly because Dale was excited to use the tools, but mostly because I was a big fat chicken who couldn't work up the nerve to ask my question.

Finally, Dale realized something wasn't quite right. "You okay, Jensen?"

"Yeah. Absolutely. Of course. Sure. Yeah." Jesus, I sounded like a teenager. I cleared my throat. "I'm fine. Why do you ask?"

The older man studied me. "Well, you're being quiet, even for you. Plus, every time I've looked up, I've found you staring at me. Not to mention...that collared shirt. A couple months ago I saw you go in and pick a t-shirt out of the hamper to wear while we were working. The whole *laundry day* argument doesn't seem to fit. So, is there something on your mind?"

This was it. My opening. He'd all but handed it to me.

"I love your daughter, Mr. Hurst."

He raised an eyebrow. "You've been calling me Dale since I asked you to ten minutes after I met you. Is there a reason why we're reverting back to formalities?"

I ran a hand through my hair. I was making a mess of this already and hadn't even gotten to the hard part. "I need to talk to you."

His eyes narrowed. "Did you do something to hurt Kenzie? Be unfaithful?"

"*What?* No. No, I would never. I wanted to talk to you about the opposite, in fact."

He stepped back from the saw and placed the wood he'd been preparing to cut to the side. "I see."

I let out a breath. "Kenzie is the most amazing woman I've ever known. I would like to ask her to marry me. But first I wanted to ask for your blessing to do so."

Dale tilted his head to the side. "Sort of an old-fashioned notion, isn't it? Asking for a father's blessing? We both know Kenzie is more than capable of making important decisions herself."

"Yes, of course. She's probably smarter than both of us combined. But I know how much you and Barbara mean to her and I just..."

I ran my hand through my hair again. Had this been a bad

idea? I hadn't meant any disrespect to either Dale or Kenzie by what I was trying to do.

This was why I had been alone for so long, because I fucked up interpersonal stuff so badly.

Dale cleared his throat. "Your relationship with your parents is strained, if I understand correctly. Is that right?"

"More like non-existent. I haven't talked to either of my parents since social service removed me from my home when I was ten."

"And before that, it wasn't a great living situation, was it?"

I rubbed my eyes. This was nothing I hadn't thought of before more than once. I couldn't blame him for bringing it up. "I know what you're getting at."

He leaned back against the saw's table. "Do you? Explain it to me."

"I know you have to be worried about me passing down my genes to any kids Kenzie and I have. My parents were abusive addicts. You probably don't want that combining with your bloodline."

"Well, I—"

"You probably have concerns that I might become an abusive addict myself."

"Actually, I—"

I couldn't blame him for that. "To be honest, I don't know that I can promise I won't. I worry about it every day. I have never touched drugs in my life, but I know that doesn't necessarily mean anything."

"Jensen—"

"You're right. This was a bad idea. I don't know what I was thinking."

"Son." He walked over and put a hand on my shoulder. "I never thought I'd have to say this to you, but I want you to be quiet now and let me talk."

Son. He'd called me *son*. I couldn't remember anyone ever calling me son to my face. I nodded.

"Have any of us ever told you how Barbara and I met?"

I shook my head.

"I went for a hike at one of our state parks when I was in grad school—literally the only hike I've ever gone on in my life. I somehow wandered off the trail and got lost. A brand-new park ranger found me and she escorted me back to my car. The rest was history."

I had to smile at that. "No, I hadn't heard the story."

"Everything about Barbara and I shouldn't work. She's outgoing, outdoorsy—big and bold and beautiful. I'm an introverted math teacher. A computer nerd. Don't think I don't know Kenzie calls me a vampire behind my back because I'm so pale."

I chuckled. "I can neither confirm nor deny that."

"I know you think you and Kenzie are opposites too."

"We are. For sure." I swallowed hard, forcing the next question out, afraid I already understood what Dale was saying. "Do you think getting married would be a mistake?"

He squeezed my shoulder. "I waited way too long to propose to Barbara because I convinced myself she wanted—*needed*—something else that wasn't me. I almost lost her because of that. What a tragedy that would've been."

I nodded, almost afraid to believe what I was hearing.

"You and Kenzie are like me and Barbara. You balance each other out. And as for your concerns about your bloodline? That's always a crapshoot. Maybe a penchant for addiction does get passed down, but the right home with two loving parents may completely change how that manifests. I guess I'm saying it's worth the risk."

"Really?" My voice came out as a whisper. I knew there were years of trauma and fear in the one word.

"Absolutely." His other hand came up to rest on my other

shoulder. "You're a good man, Jensen Chambers. Even better because of what you had to climb out of to become one. My daughter loves you to distraction and I would be delighted to have you as my son-in-law. As my son."

I wasn't a big hugger, but when the older man wrapped his arms around me, I didn't resist. "Thank you."

He thumped me on the back, then let me go. "And old fashioned or not, it means the world to me that you came to me first. You have my blessing."

"Thank you."

"We're home!" Kenzie's voice rang out and I could hear her and Barbara laughing and continuing a conversation. "Where are you guys?"

"In the workshop," I yelled, then turned to Dale. "Now I just have to convince Kenzie."

He winked at me. "Since I overheard she and her mother talking about some sort of plant conservatory in the middle of Garnet Bend and how that would be perfect for a spring wedding, it probably won't take as much convincing as you think."

I couldn't wipe the smile off my face. That would be more perfect than I'd ever imagined.

I'd be gaining a wife who I loved to distraction.

And evidently, a set of parents too.

•••••

The Resting Warrior Ranch series continues with MONTANA MEMORY

Also by Josie Jade

See more info here: www.josiejade.com

RESTING WARRIOR RANCH (with Janie Crouch)

Montana Sanctuary

Montana Danger

Montana Desire

Montana Mystery

Montana Storm

Montana Freedom

Montana Silence

Montana Rain

Montana Heat

Montana Memory

PRINCES OF FAIRYTALE, CO

Beau

www.ingramcontent.com/pod-product-compliance
Lightning Source LLC
Chambersburg PA
CBHW051145130726
47988CB00005B/1998